The
Millstone

Margaret Drabble

The Millstone

A Harvest Book

Harcourt Brace & Company

San Diego   New York   London

Requests for permission to make copies
of any part of the work should be mailed to:
Permissions Department, Harcourt Brace & Company,
6277 Sea Harbor Drive, Orlando, Florida 32887-6777.

Library of Congress Cataloging-in-Publication Data
Drabble, Margaret, 1939–
The millstone/Margaret Drabble.
p.   cm.
ISBN 0-15-600619-7
1. Man-woman relationships—England—Fiction.
2. Unmarried mothers—England—Fiction. I. Title.
PR6054.R25M55   1998
823'.914—dc21   98-20928

Printed in the United States of America
First Harvest edition 1998
F E D C B A

The
Millstone

My career has always been marked by a strange mixture of confidence and cowardice: almost, one might say, made by it. Take, for instance, the first time I tried spending a night with a man in a hotel. I was nineteen at the time, an age appropriate for such adventures, and needless to say I was not married. I am still not married, a fact of some significance, but more of that later. The name of the boy, if I remember rightly, was Hamish. I do remember rightly. I really must try not to be so deprecating. Confidence, not cowardice, is the part of myself which I admire, after all.

Hamish and I had just come down from Cambridge at the end of the Christmas term: we had conceived our plan well in advance, and had each informed our parents that term ended a day later than it actually did, knowing quite well that they would not be interested enough to check, nor sufficiently *au fait* to ascertain the value of their information if they did. So we arrived in London together in the late afternoon, and took a taxi from the station to our destined hotel. We had worked everything out, and had even booked our room, which would probably not have been necessary, as the hotel we had selected was one of those large central cheap-smart ones, specially designed for adventures such as ours. I was wearing a gold curtain ring on the relevant finger. We had decided to stick to Hamish's own name, which, being Andrews, was unmemorable enough, and less confusing than having to think up a pseudonym. We were well educated, the two of us, in the pitfalls of such occasions, having both of us read at one time in our lives a good deal of cheap fiction, and indeed we both carried ourselves with considerable aplomb. We arrived, unloaded our suitably labelled suitcases, and called at the desk for our key. It was here that I made my mistake. For some reason I was requested to sign the register: I now know that it is by no means customary for wives to sign hotel registers, and can only assume that I was made to do so because of the status of the hotel, or because I was hanging around guiltily waiting to be asked. Anyway, when I got to it, I signed it in my maiden name: Rosamund Stacey, I wrote, as large as can be, in my huge childish hand, underneath a neatly illegible Hamish Andrews. I did not even see what I had done until I handed it back to the girl, who looked at my signature, gave a sigh of irritation, and said, "Now then, what do you mean by this?"

She did not say this with amusement, or with venom, or with reprobation: but with a weary crossness. I was making work for her, I could see that at a glance: I was stopping the machinery, because I had accidently told the truth. I had meant to lie, and she had expected me to lie, but for some deeply rooted Freudian reason I had forgotten to do so. While she was drawing Hamish's attention to my error, I stood there overcome with a kind of bleak apologetic despair. I had not meant to make things difficult. Hamish got out of it as best he could, cracking a few jokes about the recentness of our wedding: she did not smile at them, but took them for what they were, and when he had finished she picked up the register and said:

"Oh, well, I'll have to go and ask."

Then she disappeared through a door at the back of her reception box, leaving Hamish and me side by side but not particularly looking at each other.

"Oh hell," I said, after a while. "I'm so sorry, dearest, I just wasn't thinking."

"I don't suppose it matters," he said.

And of course it did not matter: after a couple of minutes the girl returned, expressionless as ever, without the register, and said that that was all right, and gave us our key. I suppose my name is still there. And its inscription there in all that suspect company is as misleading and hypocritical as everything else about me and my situation, for Hamish and I were not even sleeping together, though every day for a year or so we thought we might be about to. We took rooms in hotels and spent nights in each other's colleges, partly for fun and partly because we liked each other's company. In those days, at that age, such things seemed possible and permissible: and as I did them, I thought that I was creating love and the terms of love in my own way and in my own time. I did not realize the dreadful facts of life. I did not know that a pattern forms before we are aware of it, and that what we think we make becomes a rigid prison making us. In ignorance and innocence I built my own confines, and by the time I was old enough to know what I had done, there was no longer time to undo it.

When Hamish and I loved each other for a whole year without making love, I did not realize that I had set the mould of my whole life. One could find endless reasons for our abstinence—fear, virtue, ignorance, perversion—but the fact remains that the Hamish pattern was to be endlessly repeated, and with increasing velocity and lack of depth, so that eventually the idea of love ended in me almost the day that it began. Nothing succeeds, they say, like success, and certainly nothing fails like failure.

I was successful in my work, so I suppose other successes were too much to hope for. I can remember Hamish well enough: though I cannot now quite recollect the events of our parting. It happened, that is all. Anyway, it is of no interest, except as an example of my incompetence, both practical and emotional. My attempts at anything other than my work have always been abortive. My attempt at abortion, for instance, must be a quite classic illustration of something: of myself, if of nothing else.

When, some years after the Hamish episode, I found that I was pregnant, I went through slightly more than the usual degrees of incredulity and shock, for reasons which I doubtless shall be unable to restrain myself from recounting: there was nobody to tell, nobody to ask, so I was obliged once more to fall back on the dimly reported experiences of friends and information I had gleaned through the years from cheap fiction. I never at any point had any intention of going to a doctor: I had not been ill for so many years that I was unaware even of the procedure for visiting one, and felt that even if I did get round to it I would be reprimanded like a school child for my state. I did not feel much in the mood for reproof. So I kept it to myself, and thought that I would try at least to deal with it by myself. It took me some time to summon up the courage: I sat for a whole day in the British Museum, damp with fear, staring blankly at the open pages of Samuel Daniel, and thinking about gin. I knew vaguely about gin, that it was supposed to do something or other to the womb, quinine or something, I believe, and that combined with a hot bath it sometimes works, so I decided that other girls had gone through with it, so why not me. One might be lucky. I had no idea how much gin one was supposed to consume, but I had a nasty feeling that it was a whole bottle: the prospect of this upset me both physically and financially. I grudged the thought of two pounds on a bottle of gin, just to make myself ill. However, I couldn't pretend that I couldn't afford it, and it was relatively cheap compared with other methods, so I grimly turned the pages of Daniel and decided that I would give it a try. As I turned the pages, a very handy image, thesis-wise, caught my attention, and I noted it down. Lucky in work, unlucky in love. Love is of man's life a thing apart, 'tis woman's whole existence, as Byron mistakenly remarked.

On the way home I called in at Unwin's and bought a bottle of gin. As the man handed it to me over the counter, wrapped in its white tissue paper, I wished that I were purchasing it for some more festive reason. I walked down Marylebone High Street with it, looking in the shop windows and feeling rather as though I were looking my last on the expensive vegetables and the chocolate rabbits and the cozy antiques. I would not have minded looking my last on the maternity clothes: it was unfortunate, in view of subsequent events, that the region I then inhabited was positively crammed with maternity shops and boutiques for babies, so that I could not walk down the street without being confronted by the reproachful image of a well-dressed, flat-bellied model standing and displaying with studied grace and white glass hair some chic and classy garment. The sight of them that night made me clutch the neck of my gin bottle all the more tightly, and I turned off towards the street I lived in with determination in my heart.

I was living at that time in a flat that belonged to my parents, which dangerously misrepresented my status. My parents were in Africa for a couple of years; my father had gone to a new university as professor of economics, to put them on the right track. He was on the right track himself, or he would not have been invited. They had their flat on a fifteen-year lease, and they said that while they were away I could have it, which was kind of them as they could have let it for a lot of money. They disapproved very strongly, however, of the property situation, and were unwilling to become involved in it except on a suffering and sacrificial basis: so their attitude was not pure kindness, but partly at least a selfish abstinence from guilt. I profited, anyway: it was a nice flat, on the fourth floor of a large block of an early twentieth-century building, and in very easy reach of Regent's Park, Oxford Circus, Marylebone High Street, Harley Street, and anywhere else useful that one can think of. The only disadvantage was that people would insist on assuming that because I lived there I was rather rich: which by any human standards I was, having about five hundred a year in various research grants and endowments: but this, of course, was not at all rich in the eyes of the people who habitually made such assumptions. In fact, had they known the truth they would have classed me on the starvation line, and would have ceased to make remarks about the extreme oldness of my shoes. My parents did not support me at all, beyond the rent-free accommodation, though they could have afforded to do so: but they believed in independence. They had drummed the idea of self-reliance into me so thoroughly that I believed dependence to be a fatal sin. Emancipated woman, this was me: gin bottle in hand, opening my own door with my own latchkey.

When I found myself alone in the flat, I began to feel really frightened. It seemed a violent and alarming thing to do, almost as violent and alarming as the act which had engendered this necessity, and, morever, this time I had no company. This time I was on my own. In a way that made it better: at least nobody could see. I put the bottle on the kitchen dresser with the other bottles, most of which were empty except for half an inch or so, and looked at my watch. It was half past six. I did not feel that I ought to start at half past six, and yet there did not seem to be anything else to do: I could not see myself settling down to a couple of hours' work. Nor did I think I should have anything to eat, though I was rather hungry. So I walked up and down the hall corridor for a while, and was just going into the bedroom to get undressed when the doorbell rang. I started nervously, as though caught out in an act of crime, and yet with a reprieved relief, anything being slightly better than what I was contemplating: and the people I found at the door were really quite a lot better. As soon as I saw them, I knew how very pleased I was to see them, and asked them in with cheerful goodwill.

"You weren't just about to go out, were you, Rosamund?" said Dick, walking into the kitchen and sitting on the table. "One never can tell with you. You lead such a secret life. We thought we might take you to see the new Fellini. But you probably saw it weeks ago."

"What a kind thought," I said.

"Have you seen it?" asked Lydia. "If you have, don't say a word, as I feel I want to like it, and I shan't like it if you didn't. Or if you did, come to that. So express no opinions, please."

"I haven't seen it," I said. "Where's it on?"

"At the Cameo-Poly. Regent Street."

"Oh," I said. "No, I'm not going there. I don't go down Regent Street any more."

"Why ever not?"

"I just don't, that's all," I said. It was the truth, too, and it gave me some comfort to tell them so, when they could not know the reason, or care for it had they known it.

"More of your secret life," said Dick. "Won't you really come, then?"

"No, I really won't. I've got some work to do this evening."

"Seen Mike lately?" said Dick quickly, who was always afraid, quite without precedent or reason, that I was about to lecture him on the Elizabethan sonnet sequences.

"Not for weeks," I said.

Alex, who had hitherto been silently pulling bits off a loaf of bread he was carrying, suddenly remarked:

"Why don't we all go out and have a drink "

I was well brought up. Immediately, without a second thought, I said "Oh no, why don't you have a drink here?" and as Dick, Lydia and Alex all fitted into the category of those who overrated my means, they all accepted instantly. As soon as I had said the words, I realized that they had had their eyes on my bottle of gin anyway: they had probably followed me from the shop. I poured them a glass each, and then decided that there was no point in abstaining myself, and poured another for me. Then we all went and sat down in the sitting room and talked. Dick talked about a parcel he had tried to post earlier that day, and how first the post office had said it was too heavy, and then they said the string was wrong, and then they had gone and shut while he was straightening out the string. We said what was in the parcel, and he said some bricks for his nephew's birthday. Then Lydia told us about how when she had sent off her first novel to her first publisher's she had handed it in to the post office and said politely, in her would-be modest, middle-class voice, Could I register this, please, expecting the answer Yes, certainly, ma'am: but the man had said, quite simply, No. This, too, had turned out to be a question of sealing wax and string, but she had taken it for some more prophetic assessment of her packet's worth, and had indeed been so shaken by its unexpected rejection that she had taken it back home with her and put it in a drawer for another three months. "Then," she said, "when I finally did post it off, the letter inside was three months old, so by the time they got round to reading it, it was six months old, so when I rang up after three months and told them they'd had it six months they believed me. If you see what I mean."

We didn't, quite, but we laughed, and had some more gin, and told some more stories, this time about the literary achievements of our various acquaintances. This proved a fruitful topic, as all of us there had some pretensions to writing of one kind or another, though Lydia was the only one who would have considered herself a creative artist. I myself was wholly uncreative, and spent my life on thorough and tedious collating of certain sixteenth-century poetic data, a task which enthralled me, but which was generally considered to be useless. However, I was also acknowledged to have a good critical mind in other spheres, and did from time to time a little reviewing and a good deal of reading of friends' plays and poems and novels and correspondence. Dick, for example, had entrusted to me one or two of his works, hitherto unpublished and, in my opinion, unpublishable. One was a novel, of great incidental charm and talent, but totally defective in plot and, even worse, in time scheme: I do not care very much for plots myself, but I do like to have a sequence of events. His characters had no relationship with time at all: it was impossible to tell what event preceded what, and whether a particular scene lasted for hours or days, or whether it occurred hours, days or years later than the preceding scene—or indeed perhaps before it, one simply could not tell. I pointed this out to Dick and he was startled and alarmed because he could not see what I meant, which implied that the defect must have been integral and not technical. He earned his living by writing something or other for a television company, but he was not wholly committed to his work. Alex, on the other hand, was as committed as I was: he was working for an advertising agency, writing copy, and was thoroughly enraptured by his job. He was at heart rather a serious puritanical young man, and I think it gave him great pleasure to live in such a wicked warm atmosphere, all jokes and deceitfulness, prostituting his talent. He had a great flair for copy, too, and was forever reading aloud his better slogans from stray magazines and papers. He wrote poetry on the quiet, and actually published a piece or two once every two years. Lydia was the only one who had really made it: she had published a couple of novels, but had now for some time been mooching around London moaning that she had nothing else to say. Nobody sympathized with her at all, understandably: she was only twenty-six, so what had she to worry about?

In view of her state, she seized with delight upon any stories of the atrocity of other people's latest books, of which we managed to offer a kindly few.

"It's no good, anyway," said Dick, after dismissing Joe Hurt's latest with a derisive sneer, "churning them out like that, one a year. Mechanical, that's what it is."

"A bit more mechanism wouldn't hurt you," I said gaily. I was on my second large gin.

Lydia, who had hitherto been accepting our devious comfort, suddenly turned on us with a wail of despondency.

"I don't care *what* you say," she said, "it's better to write bad books than no books, it really is. Writing nothing is—is nothing, just nothing. It's wonderful to turn out one a year, I think Joe Hurt is wonderful, I admire it, I admire that kind of thing."

"You haven't read it," said Dick.

"That's not the point," said Lydia, "it's the effort, that's the point."

"Why don't you write a bad book then?" I asked. "I bet you could write a bad book if you wanted to. Couldn't you?"

"Not if I *knew* it was bad while I was writing it. I couldn't do it. I couldn't get it done."

"What a romantic view of literary creation," said Dick.

"Speak for yourself," said Lydia crossly. "Get yours published, and then start calling me romantic. Pass the gin, Rosie, there's a darling."

"Anyway," said Alex, who had by now eaten half his loaf, "if you ask me, Joe Hurt knew quite well how bad his book was while he was writing it. It reeks of conscious badness on every page. Don't you think so, Rosie?"

"I haven't read it," I said. "But you know what Joe

always says. Nobody ever wrote a masterpiece before the age of thirty-five, Joe says, so that gives me another six years, says Joe."

"Still going out with Joe, Rosie?"

"I'm still seeing him. Do stop calling me Rosie, who gave you that idea?"

"Lydia. She called you Rosie just now."

"She likes diminishing people. It makes her feel better, doesn't it, Lyd?"

At this we all laughed loudly, and I reached for the gin and noticed with horror and dismay that it was half gone, more than half gone. Sudden pressing memories of what I had never quite forgotten came upon me, and I looked at my watch and said that wasn't it time they all went off to see their Fellini film. They were not at all easy to dislodge, having sunk down very thoroughly and chattily into my parent's extra-comfortable old deep chairs, where they had an air of being held like animals in the warmth of the central heating: they waved their arms and said they would rather stay and talk, and I almost hoped they might, and might indeed have sunk back into my chair myself, taking as ever the short-term view, the easy quiet way, when Alex suddenly had a thought. I knew what it was as soon as he sat upright and looked worried and uneasy: he thought that I had been hurt by what they had said about Hurt, as I well might have been, though in fact was not. I knew, however, as soon as I saw the reflection of this possibility upon his face, that they would go: and go they did, scrupulous as ever about personal relationships, just as they were unscrupulous about gin. I kept them talking for five minutes on the threshold, gazing anxiously from one to the other; pretty, tendril-haired Dick; hatchet-headed Alex with his stooping stork shoulders; and pale, cross, nail-chewing, eye-twitching, beautiful Lydia Reynolds, in her dirty Aquascutum mackintosh. I wondered if I could ask any of them to stay and share my ordeal, and it crossed my mind later that they would actually have enjoyed such a request, all three of them together: they would have leaped with alacrity at the prospect of such a sordid, stirring, copy-providing evening. But then, my thoughts obscured by need, I did not see it that way, and I let them go and see Fellini without me.

When they had gone I wandered back into the sitting room and sat down on the hearth rug and looked once more at the contents of my bottle of gin. There was not very much left. Not enough, I thought. Not enough, I hoped. I felt rather odd already; my head was swimming, and I felt slightly but unnaturally gay. Drink always cheers me up. I almost felt that I might abandon the whole project and go to bed instead, or cook myself some bacon and eggs, or listen to the radio: but I knew that I would have to go through with it, having once thought that I might, and regardless of its possible effectiveness. It would be so unpleasant, and I could not let myself off. So I picked up the bottle and carried it into my bedroom where I undressed, and put on my dressing gown. On my way to the bathroom I tripped over the flex of the Hoover, which had been standing in the hall all week, and missed the bathroom door knob the first time I aimed at it. I remembered that I had not eaten since lunch. But it was when I tried to run the bath that the measure of my state was brought home to me. All the hot water in the flat was run from a gas heater in the bathroom: it could be got to run at a fierce enough heat, if one managed to control the flow of the water with sufficient care: there was a very intimate relationship between the volume of water coming from the tap and the strength of the gas jet. With too much water, the temperature would drop to tepid: with too little, the gas would extinguish itself entirely and the bath would run icy cold. It was difficult enough to regulate at the best of times, but that evening I just could not get it to work at all. I sat on the bathroom stool, letting the water run, and testing it with my finger, and trying again: eventually I thought I had got it right, so I put the plug in and while I waited I drank the rest of the bottle off, neat. It was so thoroughly nasty undiluted that I felt the act of drinking was some kind of penance for the immorality of my behaviour. It had an instantaneous effect: I felt immediately so drunk that I nearly fell into the bath in my dressing gown. However, I managed to stand up and get it off and drop it on the floor: then I climbed into the water.

I climbed out again at once, for the water was stone cold. I had erred on the side of too little volume and everything had gone out but the pilot light. Shivering, I stood there and gazed, defeated, at the hot tap. Perhaps, I thought, the shock to my system would have the same effect as the heat might have done. My unnatural cheerfulness increased as I became aware of the absurdity of the situation: I managed to struggle back into my dressing gown, and then tottered back along the corridor to the bedroom, where I collapsed upon the bed. I felt so sick when I sat down that I stood up once more and decided that I would have to try to walk it off: so I walked up and down the hall and round all the rooms, and back again, and on and on and on, banging into the walls on the way. As I walked I thought about having a baby, and in that state of total inebriation it seemed to me that a baby might be no such bad thing, however impractical and impossible. My sister had babies, nice babies, and seemed to like them. My friends had babies. There was no reason why I shouldn't have one either, it would serve me right, I thought, for having been born a woman in the first place. I couldn't pretend that I wasn't a woman, could I, however much I might try from day to day to avoid the issue? I might as well pay, mightn't I, if other people had to pay? I tried to feel bitter about it all, as I usually did when sober: and indeed recently worse than bitter, positively suicidal: but I could not make it. The gin kept me gay and undespairing, and I thought that I might ring up George and tell him about it. It seemed possible then that I might. I did not have his number, or I might have rung. And there again I was trapped by that first abstinence, for having survived one such temptation to ring George, there was no reason why I should ever succumb, no reason why a point at which I could no longer bear my silence should ever arrive. Had I known my nature better then I would have rung up and found his number and told him, then and there. But I didn't. And perhaps it was better that I didn't. Better for him, I mean.

I never told anybody that George was the father of my child. People would have been highly astonished had I told them, as he was so incidental to my life that nobody even knew that I knew him. They would have asked me if I was sure of my facts. I was sure enough, having indeed a fool-proof case in favour of George's paternity, for he was the only man I had ever in my life slept with, and then only once. The whole business was utterly accidental from start to finish: in fact, one of my most painful indignations in those painful months was the sheer unlikelihood of it all. It wasn't, after all, as though I had asked for it: I had asked for it as little as anyone who had ever got it. One reads such comforting stories of women unable to conceive for years and years, but there are of course the other stories, which I have always wished to discount because of their overhanging grim tones of retribution, their association with scarlet letters, their eye-for-an-eye and Bunyanesque attention to the detail of offense. Nowadays one tends to class these tales as fantasies of repressed imaginations, and it is extraordinarily hard to convince people that it is even possible to conceive at the first attempt; though if one thinks about it, it would be odd if it were not possible. Anyway, I know it is possible, because it happened to me, as in the best moral fable for young women, and unluckily there was much in me that was all too ready to suspect it was a judgment.

Oddly enough, I never thought it was a judgment upon me for that one evening with George, but rather for all those other evenings of abstinence with Hamish and his successors. I was guilty of a crime, all right, but it was a brand-new, twentieth-century crime, not the good old traditional one of lust and greed. My crime was my suspicion, my fear, my apprehensive terror of the very idea of sex. I liked men, and was forever in and out of love for years, but the thought of sex frightened the life out of me, and the more I didn't do it and the more I read and heard about how I ought to do it the more frightened I became. It must have been the physical thing itself that frightened me, for I did not at all object to its social implications, to my name on hotel registers, my name bandied about at parties, nor to the emotional upheavals which I imagined to be its companions: but the act itself I could neither make nor contemplate. I would go so far, and no farther. I have thought of all kinds of possible causes for this curious characteristic of mine—the over-healthy, businesslike attitude of my family, my isolation (through superiority of intellect) as a child, my selfish, self-preserving hatred of being pushed around—but none of these imagined causes came anywhere near to explaining the massive obduracy of the effect. Naturally enough my virtuous reluctance made me very miserable, as it makes girls on the back page of every woman's magazine, for, like them, I enjoyed being in love and being kissed on the doorstep and, like them, I hated to be alone. I had the additional disadvantage of being unable to approve my own conduct; being a child of the age, I knew how wrong and how misguided it was. I walked around with a scarlet letter embroidered upon my bosom, visible enough in the end, but the A stood for Abstinence, not for Adultery. In the end I even came to believe that I got it thus, my punishment, because I had dallied and hesitated and trembled for so long. Had I rushed in regardless, at eighteen, full of generous passion, as other girls do, I would have got away with it too. But being at heart a Victorian, I paid the Victorian penalty.

Luckily, I paid for the more shaming details in secret. Nobody ever knew quite how odd my sexual life was and nobody, not even the men I deluded, would have been prepared to entertain the idea of my virginity. Except, of course, Hamish who, being the first, knew quite well. However, even Hamish must have assumed that I got round to it later, as he himself did. He is now married and has two children. It did not take me long to realize, however, that I couldn't have everything; if I wished to decline, I would have to pay for it. It took me some time to work out what, from others, I needed most, and finally I decided, after some sad experiments, that the one thing I could not dispense with was company. After much trial and error, I managed to construct an excellent system, which combined, I considered, fairness to others, with the maximum possible benefit to myself.

My system worked for about a year, and while it lasted it was most satisfactory; I look back on it now as on some distant romantic idyll. What happened was this. I went out with two people at once, one Joe Hurt, the other Roger Henderson, and Joe thought I was sleeping with Roger and Roger thought I was sleeping with Joe. In this way I managed to receive from each just about as much attention as I could take, such as the odd squeeze of the hand in the cinema, without having to expose myself to their crusading chivalrous sexual zeal which, had it known the true state of affairs, would have felt itself obliged for honour's sake to try to seduce me and to reveal to me the true pleasures of life. Clearly neither of them was very interested in me, or they would not have been content with this arrangement. All I had to sacrifice was interest and love. I could do without these things. Both Joe and Roger were sleeping with other girls, I suppose: Joe was reputed to have a wife somewhere, but Roger, now I come to think of it, more probably separated his sexual from his social interests. Roger was in many ways rather a nasty young man, being all that my parents had brought me up to despise and condemn; he was a wealthy well-descended Tory barrister person, clearly set for a career that would be aided more by personality than ability. He had many habits that my parents had always called vulgar, but which were no such thing, except by a total falsification of the word's meaning; for instance, he talked very loudly in public places and was uncivil to waiters who kept him waiting and people who tried to tell him about parking his car. He was not unintelligent and had a flair, connected no doubt with his profession, for picking out the main points from a book or play without reading it right through or listening to it very closely: he had a crudeness of judgment that appealed to me, as it was not ignorant, but merely impatient and unimpressed. He liked me, I think, partly because I was well-behaved and talkative, and handy to take around, but mostly because I represented for him a raffish seedy literary milieu that appealed to his desire to get to know the world. He himself appealed to exactly this same desire in me, of course; it fascinated me that such people existed. He liked the idea that I was sleeping with Joe Hurt; it gave me a seedy status in his eyes. He had a smooth face and nice suits, did Roger; his skin was like a child's, clean and well-nurtured and warm with a cool inner warmth.

Joe, too, oddly enough, liked the idea that I was sleeping with Roger, though he loathed Roger, and abused him frequently to me with violent flows of vituperative eloquence. Joe was quite the opposite from Roger, in skin texture at least: where Roger was smooth, Joe was horribly scooped and pitted and decayed, as though by smallpox. Joe was a horrific-looking person; he was well over six feet tall, and walked with a perpetual slouch, once no doubt the product of embarrassment, but now a manifestation of insolent ill-will. He was appallingly attractive: at first sight one thought him the ugliest man one had ever set eyes on, but in no time at all one found oneself considering with a quite painful admiration all the angles of his beauty. As a boy he had no doubt been ugly with an unredeemed and oppressive ugliness, and he retained many defensive aggressive symptoms from that era, but by the time I met him he must have been for years aware of his magnetic charms. As a consequence he had an attitude of defiant pleasure in his own successes: for years so unacceptable, his acceptability came to him not like Roger's as a birthright, as a given starting point, but as a challenge to be met. His wife was an American, whom he was said to have picked up while doing a couple of years over there at some university, but nobody ever saw her. He wrote novels, and since his return to England had abandoned his attempts at an academic career, and was now dabbling in films and adaptations and so forth, whilst still turning out his novel a year. His books were compulsively readable, but I felt him forever teetering on some artistic brink: he had the talent to write really well, and he maintained that one day he was going to do it, but the more efficient and readable he got the more his friends jeered and prophesied and foresaw his doom. I myself did not know what I thought about it, because his weaknesses and his strengths seemed to be so closely combined: he was naturally prolific, as I was naturally chaste. Or unnaturally, do I mean? Anyway, he would take me seriously when I made remarks (not intended seriously) like "Well, Henry James was very creative" or "Shakespeare wrote more plays than any of his contemporaries": so his desires must have been grandiose enough. It was rather touching, the way one had to cheer him up for his every success. He and Roger clearly did not know each other at all well; they had a few acquaintances in common, such as myself, and met occasionally at the more undiscriminating kind of social gathering. Each considered the other to have a kind of worldliness that was lacking in himself, and despised and revered each other accordingly. They were both right, too. I suppose Joe was far more the kind of person I might have been expected to like than Roger was, for we shared many interests, and enjoyed arguing about books and films and people and attitudes. Like Roger, he found it handy to have a second-string girl, and I found it handy to be one. It was an excellent system.

It was upon George that the whole delicate unnatural system was wrecked. Dear George, lovely George, kind and camp and unpretentious George. Thinking of George, I even now permit myself some tenderness, now so much too late. It was in Joe's company that I first met George: he was a radio announcer, and I met him very deviously in the canteen at the BBC, whither I had gone to accompany Joe, who was being interviewed about his latest work. Joe did not know George, but a friend of Joe's who was sitting at the table with us did, and he introduced us. George was at first sight rather unnoticeable, being unaggressive and indeed unassertive in manner, a quality rare enough in my acquaintance, but he had a kind of unobtrusive gentle attention that made its point in time. He had a thin and decorative face, a pleasant BBC voice and quietly effeminate clothes, and from time to time he perverted his normal speaking voice in order to make small camp jokes. Not, one might think, a dangerous or threatening character, nor one likely to inspire great passion. He had nothing, for instance, on Joe Hurt, who sat there chewing his yellow fingers with their huge buckled, cracking yellow nails, and winding his legs ferociously round the tubular steel legs of the table, while discoursing in a loudly inaudible voice about the tediousness of experimental novels. The eyes of every girl in the room kept creeping meekly and with shame back to Joe. He always had such an effect on any assembly. George listened to Joe, and he too seemed impressed, though he would make the odd-sided comment and joke, as I have said. I distinctly thought he fancied Joe. Joe attracted everyone, even those who concealed their attraction by the violence of their abuse.

After that meeting, I came across George intermittently, about once a week on an average. Sometimes in the street; living where I did, so near Broadcasting House, we were forever crossing paths in Upper Regent Street or along Wigmore Street. Sometimes we met in a pub of which he was clearly an habitué, and which Joe and I took to for a while. It was a nice pub, so I took Roger there too one night. Once we met, George and I, to our mutual surprise, at a party. I used to enjoy meeting him, because he always seemed pleased to see me, and used to make lovely remarks. "You're looking very lovely this evening, Rosamunda," he would say as I entered the Bear and Baculus, or "And how did you get on with Astrophel and Stella today?" He seemed oddly conversant with the poets; I could not place his background or education at all, which intrigued me, naturally. His accent betrayed no locality, for when it slipped from the BBC tone, it slipped not into its origins but into this universal camp parlance. There was something about his hair, oddly enough, that made one think he might not be quite as refined as he otherwise appeared. It did not lie flat, in the usual way: it had an odd sideways angle to it that made him in certain lights look almost raffish and smart. I liked it. I liked him, altogether, and after a few weeks I would persuade Joe and Roger to take me to his pub just so that I could talk to him for a few minutes.

He was very amused by the Joe-Roger alternation, and clearly thought the worst, a conclusion which gratified my pride. He would make slight clucking private noises of reproof, which amused me. I enjoyed the image of my own imaginary wickedness reflected from his eyes, for he saw what he thought he saw with so entertained an indulgence, exactly the kind of reaction I would have wanted had what he seen been true. One rather fraught summer evening I persuaded Joe to take me to the pub: we were on very bad terms, being engaged in some fruitless dispute about a pound note that we had lent or not lent to a tiresome dud friend the week before. I was very annoyed with Joe, as I have a good memory, and I distinctly remembered the whole occasion: my temper, when we reached the pub, was not improved by the fact that George did not turn up. As the time for his usual arrival passed, I grew increasingly irritable, and in the end Joe flew into a rage and walked out and left me. I sat there grimly for five minutes, pretending to finish my drink, and then I got up to go. I cannot stand sitting in pubs by myself. At the doorway I met George.

"My goodness me," he said, "all alone tonight, are you?"

"Just walked out," I said. "Joe just walked out."

"I know," he said, "I met him on Portland Place. Have another drink."

"I was just going," I said.

"Well, stay a while."

"All right," I said, "I will."

So George bought me another drink; when he came back from the bar with it he was smiling with gentle malice, and he said, "Well, all you have to do is ring up Roger. How wise you are to have your life so well organized."

"I don't like Roger much," I said, and laughed. "You don't either, do you?"

"No, I must confess that I prefer Joe. Personally," said George. And he too laughed.

"Anyway," I said, "Roger's gone on his summer holidays."

"Has he really? Amazing how people go on going on

summer holidays, don't you think? I gave it up when I was seventeen."

"How old are you now?"

"Twenty-nine."

"Like Joe."

"So Joe's gone and left you, has he? What had you been on at him about?"

"Oh, this and that," I said, and told him the story of the pound note. We talked for half an hour more, and then it began to cross my mind that he might have better things to do than to talk to me: that he didn't come into the pub to talk to me, and might well have other aims for the evening: and that he was probably spending so much time on me because he felt sorry for me being left on my own. He was a man much susceptible to the tender emotions of pity and sorrow, I suspected. As soon as these suspicions crossed my mind, they immediately seemed to me to be the simple truth, so I looked at my watch and said, "Good heavens, is that the time, I really must be going."

"Oh no, not yet," he said. "Let me get you another drink."

"No, really," I said, "I must be going, I have some work to do before the morning."

And I picked up my bag and my scarf and started fishing for my shoes which I had lost under the bench.

"I'll walk you home," he said.

"Don't be ridiculous," I said with asperity, "I only live just down the road."

"Now then, now then," he said, soothingly, "I know where you live. I didn't mean to offend you. I know you're quite capable of walking down the road by yourself. Let me walk you home."

"Why?" I said, wriggling my feet into my shoes. "Don't you want to stay and talk"—I waved my hand disparagingly around the room—"to all your friends?"

I was still not convinced that he really wanted to walk

back with me, but as I wished his company I was prepared to accept his offer without the comfort of total conviction. We set off down the broad dusty street. I was wearing a pair of rather flimsy string-backed high-heeled sandals, which kept coming off as I walked: my unsteady progress in them had not helped Joe's irritable attitude earlier in the evening. When I fell off them for the fifth time, George smiled with a mild reproof and offered me his arm. I took it and was amazed, in hanging on to it, to find how much it was there. I had never touched him before, and had always assumed he would be as insubstantial as grass, or as some thin animal: but he was there, within my grasp. I was a little shocked to find it so. He too seemed somewhat surprised, for he became silent, and we walked along without talking. When we arrived at the front door of my block of flats, we paused and I withdrew my arm with some reluctance; then I said what I had decided, marginally, not to say.

"Why don't you come up," I said, "and have a drink? Or a cup of coffee or something?"

He looked at me, suddenly very thin and fey and elusive, then said, in his most defensive tone, "Well, I don't mind if I do. That would be lovely, don't you think?"

"Yes, lovely," I said, and we went in and I opened the lift door for him, and up we went. I felt unreasonably elated and the familiar details of the building seemed to take on a sudden charm. As he followed me into the kitchen, he seemed a little subdued by the grand parental atmosphere which never quite left the place, and I had a moment of horrid fright: perhaps he wasn't quite up to it, perhaps he wasn't quite up to my kind of thing, perhaps I should never have tried to talk to him for more than five minutes, perhaps we were both about to see each other in an unpleasantly revealing social light which would finish off our distant pleasantries forever. To escape this sense of unease, I started to tell him about my parents while the kettle boiled and why they had let me have the flat, and how I couldn't for shame make money out of it by sub-letting, and how I didn't like anyone enough to let them live with me for free. "So I have to live alone, you see," I said, as I put the beans into the grinder, and hating my own tone of nervous prattle.

"You don't like being alone?" he said, and I laughed edgily and said, "Well, who does?"

"Oh, quite," he said, "quite. We're all human, I suppose," and I looked at him and saw that it was all right after all.

"You seem to look after yourself, though," he said as I poured the water into the pot. "You seem to keep yourself quite busy."

"I try my best," I said, and we carried the tray back into the sitting room. "And what about you?" I said as we sat down, I in one of the armchairs and he on the settee.

"What do you mean?" he said, "what about me?"

"Tell me about you."

"What about me?" he said, smiling a deprecating smile, and shrugging his shoulders elaborately with a feminine emphatic diffidence.

"All about you," I said with real avidity, for at that moment I so much wanted to know, I wanted to know all about him, being interested, caught, intent: but he continued to smile evasively and said:

"What do you mean, all?"

"Well," I said, "where do you come from?"

"Ipswich," he said.

"I don't know anything about Ipswich."

"I bet you don't even know where it is."

"Oh yes I do. It's sort of over there," and I waved my hand meaninglessly at an imaginary map of England, sketched on the drawing-room air. He continued in this vein, telling me nothing at all, but telling it with such an air of confidence that I did not take it amiss: I did not quite dare to ask him about what his father did, or any such pertinent questions, though now I wish to God that I had had more courage, and had kept him at it until I had found out the lot. He resisted the pressure of my interest with expert skill, and this in itself surprised me as I was so used to being given endless unsolicited confidences by those in whom I had no interest at all. It occurred to me then that perhaps alone of my acquaintances he was not entirely obsessed by the grandeur of his soul or his career. He was an unassertive man. The very course of his career, which was all that emerged with any clarity, seemed to prove this: he had been sent to Hong Kong on his National Service, where he had got himself involved with Overseas Broadcasting, and on leaving had stayed on with the BBC, moving round the Middle East for a couple of years and then returning to London. When I asked him if it was boring, announcing boring things day in and day out, he said yes, but that he liked being bored. So I said that something must interest him, then, if his work didn't, and he said yes, I did, so why not talk about me.

I tried to match him in diffidence but, of course, could not manage it. He asked me about my family, a subject on which I found it easy enough to be truthful: I recounted in some detail their extraordinary blend of socialist principle and middle-class scruple, the way they had carried the more painful characteristics of their non-conformist inheritance into their own political and moral attitudes.

"They have to punish themselves, you see," I said. "They can't just let things get comfortable. All this going to Africa and so on, other people don't do it, other people just say they ought to do it, but my parents, they really go. It was the same with the way they brought us up, they were quite absurd, the way they stuck to their principles, never asking us where we'd been when we got back at three in the morning, sending us to state schools, having everything done on the National Health, letting us pick up horrible cockney accents, making the charlady sit down and dine with us, introducing her to visitors, all that kind of nonsense. My God, they made themselves suffer. And yet at the same time they were so nice, so kind, so gentle, and people aren't nice and kind and gentle, they just aren't. The charlady went off with all the silver cutlery in the end, she despised them, I could see her despising them, and she knew they wouldn't take any steps. And the awful thing is that they weren't even shocked when she did it, they had seen it coming, they said. And my brother went and married a ghastly girl whose father was a colonel, and now he lives in Dorking and spends all his time having absolutely worthless people to dinner and playing bridge. My sister still tries, but she married a scientist and they live on the top of a hill in the middle of the country on a housing estate near an atomic station, and last time I went she was stopping the kids from playing with the kids next door because they'd taught them to say Silly Bugger. It's been a disastrous experiment in education, that's all one can call it."

"Except for you," said George.

"What do you mean, except for me? I don't consider myself to be a very fine example of anything."

"Aren't your parents glad you've gone in for scholarship?"

"Oh no, not really. Oh, I suppose they're pleased in a way that I did so well, but they think I'm a dilettante, I mean to say, Elizabethan sonnet sequences, it isn't as though I were even doing nineteenth-century novels or something worthy like that. They wanted me to read economics at Cambridge, or at least history. They never said so, but I could tell. There's no moral worth in an Elizabethan sonnet sequence, you know."

"They must approve, though, of your independence."

I looked at him uneasily, not sure whether he meant this straight or as a crack of some kind.

"Won't you have a drink?" I said. "Have a whisky or something."

"Don't they, though?"

"I'm not at all sure that I am at all independent," I said, getting up and going to switch on the radio. "But I would like to be, that's true. Because, who knows, one may have to be."

There was some Mozart on the Third; I left it on.

"Aren't you working this evening?" I said. "Aren't you supposed to be there, doing a bit of announcing?"

"Not tonight. It is Friday, isn't it? Why, do you want me to go?"

"No, not at all. I like you to stay. If you like to stay."

And I stood there by the radio, looking at him, and he looked back, and seemed to indicate, though not precisely, that I should go and sit by him on the settee. So I did, and he took my hand and held it, and then started to kiss my fingers, one by one. After a while I remembered what was at the back of my mind, and I said, "My mother, you know, was a great feminist. She brought me up to be equal. She made there be no questions, no difference. I was equal. I am equal. You know what her creed was? That thing that Queen Elizabeth said about thanking God that she had such qualities that if she were turned out in her petticoat in any part of Christendom, she would whatever it was that she would do. She used to quote that to us, when we were frightened about exams or going to dances. I have to live up to her, you know."

And I in my turn raised his hand to my lips: it was so beautiful and cool and thin a hand, and I kissed it with some sadness. At the touch of my mouth, he took me in his arms and kissed me all over the face, and eventually we subsided gently together and lay there quietly. Knowing that he was queer, I was not frightened of him at all, because I thought that he would expect no more from me, and I was so moved and touched and pleased by the thought that he might like me, by the thought that he found me of interest. I was so happy for that hour that we lay there because truly I seemed to see him through the eyes of love, so irrationally valuable did he seem. I look back now with some anguish to each touch and glance, to every changing conjunction of limbs and heads and hands. I have lived it over every day for so long now that I am in danger of forgetting the true shape of how it was, because each time I go over it I wish that I had given a little more here or there, or at the very least said what was in my heart, so that he could have known how much it meant to me. But I was incapable, even when happy, of exposing myself thus far.

After a while the radio closed down on us, and we were left there in silence, except for the hum of the machine. I started to pull myself upright and said, "I must go and switch that thing off, I can't stand that noise," but he held on to me and said, "No, don't go." I pulled away and said that I must, and before I knew where I was I found myself thinking that I couldn't stop him if he really wanted to, because I liked him so much, and if I stopped him he would believe that I didn't: also that if ever, now: also that it would be good for me. So I shut my eyes, very tight, and waited. It was quite simple, as it was summer and I was wearing very few clothes, and he seemed to know quite well what he was doing: but then of course so did I *seem* to know, and I didn't. However, I managed to smile bravely, in order not to give offense, despite considerable pain, and I hoped that the true state of affairs would not become obvious. I remember that he stroked my hair, just before, and said in his oh so wonderfully polite and chivalrous way:

"Is this all right? Are you all right, will this be all right?"

I knew what he meant and, eyes shut, I smiled and nodded, and then that was it and it was over. Which proves that deception is indeed a tangled web. And I had no one but myself to blame. But it was something that when I opened my eyes again, there was only George: I clutched his head to my bosom and I cried:

"Oh George, tell me about you, tell me about you," but now it was his turn to shut his eyes and, moaning softly, he buried his face against me while I stroked his hair and the thin brown hollow of his cheek. After a while he did say something which, though hardly distinguishable, I took to be "Oh God, how pointless this is." I was a little perturbed by this statement, though not so much then as later, and after a couple more minutes I got up, switched off the radio, and went off to the bathroom, leaving him enough time to straighten himself up or even, if he so wished, to disappear. I returned, some time later, in my dressing gown, and found him still there, sitting where I had left him, but now upright and with his eyes open.

"Hello," I said, stopping in the doorway and smiling brightly, willing to show anything rather than the perplexing mass of uncertainties which possessed me.

"Hello, George, what about a drink?"

"I wouldn't mind a drink," said George, so off I went into the kitchen and came back with a bottle of whisky, or what was left of it, and we both had a large drink. I sat on the floor with my back against his knees, which gave me a sense of touch without contact that I found extremely comforting. He rested one hand heavily on my head, which was comforting too. I drank the drink quickly, and felt a little better. After all, I said to myself, people don't do that to other people just because they think they ought to. Just through sheer politeness because they think they've been invited in to do it. People don't work like that, I said to myself. He must have wanted it a bit. I told myself, or he wouldn't have bothered. However kind he appears to be, he can't be as kind as all that. He must be one of these bisexual people, I thought, or perhaps even he's no more queer than I am promiscuous, or whatever the word is for what I pretend to be. Perhaps we appeal to each other because we're rivals in hypocrisy.

After some time, George said:

"Rosamund, I ought to be going."

"Ought you?" I said.

"I think so."

Thinking that he probably wanted to go, I did not quite know whether I ought to suggest that he might stay, for once I had suggested it, kindness and chivalry might have kept him against his will. So I said nothing, but sat there for a moment more, feeling the weight of his hand upon my head, hot and warm and enclosing, like being all of me held in it, and feeling that there was no way to stay there in this momentary illusory safety. Then I stood up and said that it was late, I hoped it was not too late, and that I hoped he would get back where he was going. And even then, even at that moment, I did not have the courage to ask him where he lived, or to ask him what his phone number was, for it would have seemed an intrusion, an assumption that I had a right to know, that a future existed where it would be of use to know. I see, oh yes I see that my diffidence, my desire not to offend looks like enough to coldness, looks like enough to indifference, and perhaps I mean it to, but this is not what it feels like in my head. But I cannot get out and say, Where do you live, give me your number, ring me, can I ring you? In case I am not wanted. In case I am tedious. So I let him go, without a word about any other meeting, though he was the one thing I wanted to keep: I wanted him in my bed all night, asleep on my pillow, and I might have had him, but I said nothing. And he said nothing. He could have done. He could have said, when can I see you again? But he didn't. It may be that I manifested enough strangeness and indifference to prevent him. It may be that he did not wish to, which, being the most unpleasant conclusion, was the one that I most readily believed. Or it may have been that, like me, he did not wish to make assumptions.

When he had gone, I went to bed and lay there for some time thinking over what we had said and done. I could not get to sleep. For the first hour I was more happy than not, but as the night wore on and I came no nearer to sleep my mind became wracked by suspicion and by doubt. It was not that I felt guilt or regret for the one irreversible thing that had happened: about that I continued to feel nothing but relief. But such things do not happen in the abstract, and the circumstances worried me. I went back over every word George had said, and the more I looked back, the clearer it seemed that he had expressed no liking or affection for me at all. He had said I interested him, but he had said that only as a ploy, as a gambit. And anyway, what ground was interest on which to enact the event that had taken place? As I tossed and turned and tried to find a cool place for my cheek on the pillow, it became increasingly clear to me that he had made no overture at all: that I myself had made the decisive move, in going to sit next to him on the settee after switching on the radio, and that what I had taken to be a look inviting me to do just that had probably been nothing of the sort. I had offered myself, and thinking what he did of me he had accepted, through kindliness or curiosity or embarrassment; not in any case through anything like the tender emotions that had prompted me. The more I thought of it, the more hopeless it seemed: had he liked me, he would surely have made some suggestion that he might see me again?

I ended up by convincing myself, almost, that the worst must be true: yet at the same time I knew it was not true, I knew that he would ring me, and that he had liked me, and that he would be happy to go on liking me. But I had to prepare for the worst. I did not wish to be deceived, I did not wish to be taken by surprise.

George did not ring. After a week I knew that he was not going to, and I abandoned the idea. I could have seen him, easily enough, by calling at his pub or even by walking down Portland Place and Upper Regent Street on the off-chance, at some likely hour, but pride restrained me. If he does not want to see me, I thought, I do not want to see him. So I kept resolutely away from anywhere where I might be remotely likely to bump into him: I even took a different route to the British Museum each morning, and on one occasion when I was obliged to accompany a friend along Wigmore Street I found myself trembling with fearful expectation. But it is easy to avoid people in London, and I managed it well enough. The geography of the locality took on, however, a fearful moral significance: it became a map of my weaknesses and my strengths, a landscape full of petty sloughs and pitfalls, like the one which Bunyan traversed. I avoided each place where we had ever met, and each place which I had even heard him mention: one day I found myself pretending that I was obliged to go and buy a certain article from Peter Robinson's on Oxford Circus, and I only just caught myself out in time. I stuck to it and, of course, as the week lengthened into a fortnight, and the fortnight into a month, it became increasingly impossible to change my line of retreat.

It took me some time to realize that I was pregnant: the possibility had of course crossed my mind fairly early on, but I had dismissed it as being too ridiculous and unlikely a symptom of my sense of doom to be worth serious attention. When I was finally obliged to acknowledge my condition, I was for the first time in my life completely at a loss. I remember the moment quite well: I was sitting at my usual desk in the British Museum looking up something on Sir Walter Raleigh, when out of the blue came this sudden suspicion, which hardened instantly as ever into a certainty. I got out my diary and started feverishly checking on dates, which was difficult as I never make a note of anything, let alone of trivial things like the workings of my guts. In the end, however, after much hard memory work, I sorted it out and convinced myself that it must be so. I sat there, and I could see my hand trembling on the desk. And for the first time the prospect before me seemed so appalling that even I, doom-suspecting and creating as I have always been, could not look at it. It was an unfamiliar sensation, the blankness that occupied my mind instead of the usual profuse images of disaster. I remained in this state for some five minutes before, wearily, I set my imagination to work. What it produced for me was very nasty. Gin, psychiatrists, hospitals, accidents, village maidens drowned in duck ponds, tears, pain, humiliations. Nothing, at that stage, resembling a baby. These shocking forebodings occupied me for half an hour or more, and I began to think that I would have to get up and go, or to go out and have a cup of coffee or something. But it was an hour before my usual time for departure, and I could not do it. I so often wanted not to do my full three hours, and had so often resisted the lure of company or distraction in order to complete them, that now I felt myself compelled to sit there, staring at the poems of Sir Walter Raleigh, in a mockery of attention. Except that after some time I found myself really attending: my mind, bent from its true obsession with what seemed at first intolerable strain, began to revert almost of its own accord to its more accustomed preoccupations, and by the end of the morning I had covered exactly as much ground as I had planned. It gave me much satisfaction, this fact. Much self-satisfaction. And as I walked down the road to meet Lydia for lunch, I discovered another source of satisfaction: now, at least, I would be compelled to see George. I had an excuse, now, for seeing him.

Later that afternoon I realized that I was going to see George now less than ever. It took some time for the full complexity of the situation to sink in. When I realized the implications of my deceit, it became apparent that I was going to have to keep the whole thing to myself. I could not face the prospect of speculation, anyone's speculation. So I decided to get on with it by myself as best I could. I have already recounted my ludicrous attempt with the gin: after this I got in touch with a Cambridge friend of mine who had had an abortion, and asked for the address and details, which I obtained. I rang the number once, but it was engaged. After that I went no further. I do not like to look back on those first months, before anyone but me knew what was happening: it seemed too much like a nightmare, like an hallucination, and I kept waking up each morning and thinking it must be a dream, the kind of dream that my non-conformist guilt might be expected to project: I even wondered if all the symptoms from which I suffered might not be purely psychological. In the end it was the fear of being made a fool of by my subconscious that drove me to the doctor.

Seeing the doctor was not as simple an operation as one might have supposed. To begin with, I did not know which doctor to see. It was so many years since I had been unwell that I did not know how to set about it: in fact, I had not been unwell since I had become an adult. I had never had to do it on my own. The only doctor I knew was our old family doctor, who lived near our old but now abandoned family residence in Putney, and he was clearly unsuitable. I supposed that I ought to go to the nearest GP, but how was I to know who he was, or where he lived? living within two minutes' walk of Harley Street as I did, I was terrified that I might walk into some private waiting room by accident, and be charged fifty guineas for what I might and ought to get for nothing. Being my parents' daughter, the thought outraged me morally as well as financially. On the other hand, it did not seem a good plan to pick a surgery so evidently seedy that it could not exist but on the National Health: though this was in fact what I did. I passed one day, in a small road off George Street, after visiting an exhibition by a very distant friend, a brass plaque on a front door that said Dr. H. E. Moffatt. There was a globular light over the door, with SURGERY painted on it in black letters. It was not the kind of door behind which anyone could be charged fifty guineas, and I made a note of the surgery hours and resolved to return the next day at five-thirty.

I visited the doctor the next day. That visit was a revelation: it was an initiation into a new way of life, a way that was thenceforth to be mine forever. An initiation into reality, if you like. The surgery opened at five-thirty, and I made a point of going along there quite promptly: I arrived at about twenty-eight minutes to six, thinking that I was in plenty of time, and would have to wait hardly at all. But when I opened that shabby varnished door, I found a waiting room overflowing with waiting patients, patiently waiting. There were about twenty of them, and I wavered on the threshold, thinking I might change my mind, when a woman in a white nylon overall came in and said irritably:

"Come on, come along in now and don't leave the door on the jar, it's on the bell, it makes a dreadful noise in the back."

Meekly, I stepped in and shut the door behind me. I had no idea what I ought to do next: whether I should sit down, or give my name to somebody, or what. I felt helpless, exposed, before those silent staring rows of eyes. I stood there for a moment, and then the woman in white, who had been talking to a very old man sitting almost on top of the noisy gas fire, came over to me and said, in a tone of deliberate strained equanimity:

"Well, are you here to see Dr. Moffatt? You're a new patient, aren't you?"

"Yes," I said.

"Have you brought your National Health card?"

"Oh no, I quite forgot, I'm frightfully sorry," I said with shame; I had known that I would make some mistake in procedure. I did not know the ropes.

"Oh dear me," she said, and sighed heavily. "Do remember to bring it along next time, won't you? What's your name?"

"Stacey," I said. "Rosamund Stacey."

"Mrs. or Miss?"

"Miss."

"All right then, take a seat."

"As a matter of fact," I said, "I do know the *number* on my National Health card, if that's any use."

"Oh, do you really?" She brightened faintly at the news of this extraordinary feat of memory, and I reeled it off, glad to have helped, but rather confused by my eccentricity. I had been forced to learn the number by a ferocious matron at school when I had forgotten to take my card along to one of those routine knee-knocking inspections to which schoolgirls are periodically subjected. I had never since had occasion to use it. Everything comes in some day, I suppose. She noted it down, and said once more "Do take a seat," then disappeared behind a small hardboard partition in a corner of the room. I tried to follow her advice but there was not a space left: I was preparing to prop myself up against the wall by the door when two women shuffled up along the bench to make a grudging gap for me. I sat down and prepared to wait.

I waited for one hour fourteen minutes precisely: I timed it. And during that time I had plenty of leisure to observe my companions in endurance. The people that I was used to seeing on my home ground were a mixed enough lot, but they were a smart, expensive mixed lot, apart from the occasional freak, beggar or road worker: but here, gathered in this room, were representatives of a population whose existence I had hardly noticed. There were a few foreigners; a West Indian, a Pakistani, two Greeks. There were several old people, most of them respectably shabby, though one old woman was worse than shabby. She was grossly fat and her clothes were held around her by safety pins: a grostesquely old and mangy fur coat fell open to reveal layers of fraying, loose-stitched, hand-knitted cardigans in shades of maroon, dark blue and khaki. Her legs, covered in thick lisle stockings, were painfully swollen, and overflowed at the ankles over her soft cracked flat black shoes. She was talking to herself all the time, a low pitiable monologue of petty persecution. Nobody listened. Then there were a couple of young secretaries or waitresses who were sitting together and looking at pictures in a magazine and giggling: my eyes kept going back to them as they were the only people in the room who did not look depressed and oppressed. Those who looked worst of all were, ominously enough, the mothers: there were four mothers there with young children, and they looked uniformly worn out. One held a small baby on her knee, at which she smiled from time to time with tired affection and anxiety. The others had larger children, two of which were romping around the room; they were doing no harm, apart from disturbing the magazines, and nobody minded them except their mothers, who kept grabbing them and slapping them and shouting at them in a vain and indeed provoking effort to make them sit down and keep quiet. It was a saddening sight. I wondered where all the others had gone: the bright young women in emerald green coats with fur collars, the young men in leather jackets, the middle-aged women with dogs on leads, the gay mothers with their Christopher Robin children, the men with umbrellas against the rain. Sitting in Harley Street, no doubt, just along the road.

By the time my turn to see the doctor came, my complaint seemed so trivial in comparison with the ills of age and worry and penury that I had doubts about presenting it at all. Reason told me, however, that I must do so, and I did. The woman in white showed me into the surgery: Dr. Moffatt was a harassed, keen-looking young man, with pale ginger receding hair. I felt sorry for him: he must have had a more unpleasant hour and a quarter than I had had. He told me to sit down and asked me what he could do for me, and I said that I thought I was pregnant, and he said how long had I been married, and I said that I was not married. It was quite simple. He shook his head, more in sorrow than in anger, and said did my parents know. I said Yes, thinking it would be easier to say yes, and not wishing to embark on explaining about their being in Africa. He said were they sympathetic, and I smiled my bright, meaningless smile and said Fairly. Then we worked out dates and he said it would be due in March. Then he said he would try to get me a hospital bed, though I must understand there was a great shortage, and this and that, and had he got my address. I gave it, and he said was I living with my family and I said No, alone. He said did I know about the Unmarried Mothers people in Kentish Town, and I said Yes. They were very nice and very helpful about adoption and things, he said. Then he said that he would let me know about the hospital bed, and would I come back in a fortnight. And that was that.

I walked out into the cold evening air and wandered aimlessly up towards Marylebone Road, worrying not because it seemed that I was really going to have this baby, but because I had been so surprised and annoyed that I had to wait so long. Everyone else there had looked resigned; they had expected to wait, they had known they would have to wait. I was the only one who had not known. I wondered on how many other serious scores I would find myself ignorant. There were things that I had not needed to know, and now I did need to know them. I emerged upon Marylebone Road and walked towards the lovely coloured gleaming spire of Castrol House. I felt threatened. I felt my independence threatened: I did not see how I was going to get by on my own.

Once I had thus decided to have the baby—or rather failed to decide not to have it—I had to face the problem of publicity. It was not the kind of event one can conceal forever, and I was already over three months gone. The absence of my parents was certainly handy from that point of view: there was nobody else in the family that I saw at all regularly. My brother in Dorking I saw dutifully about once every four months, but he would be easy enough to evade. My sister, on the other hand, I thought I might tell at some point as she had three children of her own and I thought she might be sympathetic. We got on quite well together, as sisters go. Nevertheless, I delayed writing; I could not bear the idea of the fuss. I hate to cause trouble.

My own friends were another matter. I simply could not make my mind up about Joe and Roger; I did not much fancy going around with them while expecting somebody else's child, nor did I think they would much fancy it themselves, though one can never tell. On the other hand, I did not relish the thought of all the spare evenings I would be left with if I disposed of them both. It was difficult enough to keep myself from getting depressed as it was, without having even more solitary time on my hands. Also, I did not know quite how to set about imparting the news: should I leave it till it became evident to the naked eye? Surely not. Therefore I would have to tell them before it became evident, which did not leave me much time. Already I could not fasten my skirts or get into my brassières. I rehearsed each scene a hundred times in my head, but could never even in my imagination manipulate the data with anything like grace, skill, tact or credit to myself. I thought Joe would be the easier proposition, being more familiar, and I plunged into the subject one night almost unintentionally, prompted by a chance remark of his made as we were walking along Park Lane.

"Did you ever see," he said, "that Bergman film about a maternity ward? The one where all the wrong people kept having miscarriages?"

"Don't talk to me about maternity wards," I said, almost without thinking.

"Why not?" he said. "Does it upset you? You don't like all that kind of thing, do you? A very unwomanly woman, that's what you are."

"Nonsense," I said. "Just don't talk about maternity wards that's all. All too soon I'm going to find myself in one."

"What?" said Joe.

"I'm pregnant," I said crossly.

"Oh," said Joe, and kept on walking. After a few yards he said, "You're not going to have it, are you?"

"Yes, I am," I said.

"Whatever for?"

"Why not? I don't see why I shouldn't, do you?"

"I can think of a hundred reasons why you shouldn't. I think it's an utterly ridiculous romantic stupid nonsensical idea. I think you're out of your mind."

"I don't see why," I stubbornly repeated.

"What does he say, anyway?" continued Joe. "It's his fault, it's his job to get you out of it. He's rich enough, isn't he? Why don't you make him pay and go off and have it done in comfort?"

"Roger, you mean," I said faintly.

"Well, yes, Roger. Why don't you get married? No, for God's sake, don't bother to tell me. I can't imagine anyone wanting to marry a selfish well-dressed lump of mediocrity like him. Still if you don't marry him, you might as well do something about it."

"I don't want to do anything about it."

"Don't tell me you *want* to have a baby."

"I don't mind," I said.

"What does he think about it, anyway? If he does think."

"I haven't told him yet," I said truthfully.

"You haven't told him? You really must be out of your mind. Whyever not?"

"I just haven't got round to it."

"Oh Christ. I give up. What have you done about it?"

"I went to the doctor," I said with some pride, "and he's booking me a hospital bed."

"God," he said to himself, staring up at the black sky through the neon-lit trees, "she means it, she's going to have it." He was rattled, poor Joe; I could feel him being rattled. He didn't like the idea at all.

"You can't," he said, after another few yards of silence. "You just can't. I forbid you. It'll ruin your life. If you want some money, I'll lend you some. How much do you want? A hundred? Two hundred? How much do you need?"

"Thank you very much, Joe." I said, touched, "but I don't need anything. It's too late now, anyway."

I said this with some authority, though I did not know the facts, as I had not known the facts about gin or doctor's waiting rooms; but he did not know the facts either and he believed me.

"Oh well," he said, "if you want to make a fool of yourself. Don't tell me, you've probably been longing to have a baby all your life. You won't be able to keep it, though. They won't let you keep it. So you'll go and get yourself all upset about nothing, the whole thing'll be a complete waste of time and emotion."

I could not work out my response to this immediately, as I was highly offended by both its implications: first, that I was the kind of person who had always had a secret yearning for maternal fulfilment, and second, that some unknown authority would start interfering with my decisions by removing this hypothetical child. I decided to tackle the first one first.

"Of course I haven't always been longing to have a baby," I said, "I can't think of anything that has ever crossed my mind less. The thought of a baby leaves me absolutely stone cold."

"Nonsense," said Joe. "All women want babies. To give them a sense of purpose."

"What utter rubbish," I said, with incipient fury, "what absolutely stupid reactionary childish rubbish. Don't tell me that any human being ever endured the physical discomforts of babies for something as vague and pointless as a sense of purpose."

"What does it feel like?" said Joe, momentarily distracted.

"Nothing much. One can't really tell much difference," I replied untruthfully. "Yet."

"Anyway," said Joe, "so I believe you, so you've never thought much about having babies, but just the same, I bet you'd be pretty annoyed if somebody told you you couldn't have one, wouldn't you?"

"Not at all," I said staunchly, "I would be highly relieved. There is nothing that I would rather hear." Though, as a matter of fact, he was quite right and I was in some perverse and painful way quite proud of my evident fertility.

"In that case," said Joe, "I don't see why you didn't have something done about it."

I was silent because I did not see why not either. We had by this time reached Marble Arch: there had been a suggestion at an earlier point in the evening that Joe should here catch the tube home, and we paused by its entrance, and I said:

"Well, I think we ought to stop going around together, or whatever it is that we do."

"Why?" said Joe.

A complete silence fell, and I suddenly felt quite over-come with weakness and misery. At that moment I could not envisage any kind of future at all, and the complete lack of any sense of control or direction scared and alarmed me. All I knew was that I must get rid of Joe quick, before he sensed my poverty, because even Joe was capable of pity and of kindness.

"I don't know why," I said brightly. "I just don't kind of fancy the idea of going out much any more. Anyway, think how embarrassing it would be, taking around a preg-nant woman. Everyone would think it was yours, wouldn't they, and get on at you about it. You know how incredu-lous people are of the finer points of any relationship."

"You'd better tell Roger," said Joe, staring moodily at the ground.

"As a matter of fact," I said, thinking that however con-venient I really could not allow this misapprehension to flourish, "it isn't Roger's."

"Not Roger's?"

"No. Not Roger's."

"Oh."

"So you see, things aren't quite what they might be." I made this remark with a wealth of bogus implication that must have convinced him completely, because all he said was, "Oh well, I do see." Which in the nature of things he could not possibly have done. However, on the basis of this totally meaningless understanding he took my hand and gave it a fatherly squeeze and said:

"Look after yourself, anyway, Rosamund."

"Oh, I will," I said.

"I suppose we'll see each other around, anyway."

"Yes, I suppose so."

And so we parted. As I walked home, I wondered what he could possibly have imagined the real situation to be, as the truth itself was far too unlikely, far too veiled by de-ception to hit upon: perhaps, I finally concluded, he had thought that I had another permanent man about, whom I refused to marry or discuss through some perfectly characteristic quirk of principle. I hoped that he had thought that. It was the kindest conclusion to my vanity and to his.

Having thus successfully disposed of Joe, I knew I would have to dispose of Roger. I relished this task even less than the former one, for whereas Joe and I shared a certain area of moral background, Roger and I shared nothing at all. As it turned out, however, the evening on which I divulged my state to him was far pleasanter than the one I had spent with Joe, which had been marked by rather too much walking and chilly night air. Roger did not believe in walking: he would drive for miles and miles round his destination looking for parking places rather than park five minutes' walk away and continue on foot. I did not approve of this, being made of sterner stuff myself, but I enjoyed it.

On the evening in question, we had been to a cocktail party at Earls Court, given by some businesslike friend of Roger's: the drink was far too strong and after a couple of glasses I actually began to feel rather faint. Roger, being a gentleman born, soon noticed my pallor and the glassy look with which I was countering a young man who was telling me in great detail about the joys of accountancy, and he arrived to my rescue instantly and removed me to his car, which was waiting just outside the front door of the house. I sat there for a few minutes and then felt better: I felt cheerful enough in the first place because of the drink, and as soon as my ears stopped buzzing I felt quite splendid.

"Feeling better?" said Roger, as he noticed me perking up.

"Much better," I said.

"What's the matter with you?"

"Nothing," I said. "I was probably just hungry, I didn't have much for lunch."

"Let's go and have dinner," said Roger.

"All right," I said, though as a matter of fact the prospect made me once more feel slightly queasy as Roger had a passion for highly elaborate food of the most indigestible kind: usually I survived it quite well physically though I doubted if I would tonight, but it always gave me moral qualms. My misgivings became stronger when he said:

"There's a new place in Frith Street that someone was telling me about the other day. I thought we might try it."

I nodded and tried to look pleased, and as we drove past the lighted windows of Harrods I summoned up my courage and said,

"What nationality?"

"What nationality what?" said Roger, trying to beat a car of his own make to the lights, and making it, thank goodness.

"What nationality *food?*" I said.

"I'm not sure," he said, "but they said it was quite clean. For foreigners."

He made this remark with an impassive countenance: I was quite unable to tell whether such remarks were straight or intended as jokes, or even intended as attacks upon my ridiculous notions of liberal equality. He was always making such ambiguous statements about subjects like black men, money, modern art and so forth: on the whole I think they were meant to provoke, but I never rose as I was always too amazed to react at all. Nobody else that I had ever known had made remarks like those: it was a continual surprise to me that he could make them and yet at the same time like me enough to pay for my dinners.

The restaurant turned out to be French, and rather flashy. The tables were too close together. Roger had mussels and some infinitely messed-about steak. I had vegetable soup and grilled sole and mashed potatoes and even so I did not feel too good by the end of it. Then Roger started thinking about having crêpes suzette, and tried to persuade me to have some too, as they made it for two, but I simply could not face it. It was quite a novelty for me to feel so doubtful, as until then I had always had a cast-iron constitution, and on the rare occasions when I had suffered, I had suffered with good will. Roger would not let the topic of crêpes suzette drop but went on about them quite mercilessly, and I felt sudden retrospective insight into the plight of all those whom in the past I had sneered at for delicacy of health and appetite. In the end I said:

"It's no good, Roger, I just don't feel well," and he set about ordering crêpes for one. When he had dealt with the waiter he turned back to me and said, "What's the matter with you, then?"

"I'm pregnant," I said, hoping that the American lady at the next table was not at that moment listening to us, as she had been for most of our meal.

"I thought perhaps you might be," said Roger, and poured himself a little more claret.

"You what?" I said, in genuine astonishment.

"Well, I mean to say, and don't think I'm being rude, my dear, but you are beginning to look a little bit that way . . . that dress, for instance."

"I did wonder," I said, "when I put it on. But it's the only one I've got that does for your horrid friends."

"Don't insult my friends," said Roger equably; "look at what your horrid friends have done, and to a nice girl like you too. That's what comes of mixing with all those nasty artists."

"It's not really very noticeable, is it?" I said anxiously.

"Oh no. I only noticed it myself this evening. And with your feeling off-colour too. Have a drink, I should think you need it."

"No," I said. "I do need it, but it makes me feel awful."

"Oh look," said Roger, "here they come with my crêpe mixture. Let's just sit quietly and watch the flames."

So we sat and watched the flames, and when Roger had with great satisfaction finished eating he turned his attention back to me, and said:

"Well, what are you going to do about it, if that's not too tiresome a question?"

"Nothing," I said.

"Nothing at all?"

"Nothing at all."

"You're going to let nature take its course?"

"That's right."

"Well, well," said Roger. "What a brave girl you are."

"It might be quite nice to have a baby," I said, thinking that if I said this to everybody for the next six months I might convince both myself and them.

"My dear girl," said Roger, "it's not quite as easy as all that, you know. It's quite a performance, having a baby. And then what do you do with it when you've got it?"

"Keep it," I said.

"What on? Is he going to support you? I don't suppose for a moment that he is, and you couldn't possibly keep a child on what you've got."

"People," I said, "bring up families of four on ten pounds a week."

"Nonsense," said Roger. Though it wasn't nonsense.

Our discussion paused for a while as our coffee arrived and was poured out. While he was stirring in his sugar, he said, "You don't feel like getting married, do you?"

"Not particularly," I said. "In fact, not at all."

"That's a pity," he said, "because I thought you might like to marry me."

"Good heavens, Roger," I said, touched and impressed,

"how extremely noble of you. How lucky for you that I declined before you offered."

"We could always get divorced more or less instantly," he said.

"I don't see that that would do any good to anyone," I said. "Think of your career."

"That's true," said Roger. "Still, it would have its compensations."

"I can't think of any," I said. "I think it's a ridiculous notion. But nice, just the same."

"Good," he said. "I'm glad you liked it."

And there our conversation seemed to rest as I could not think how to continue it: the thought of marrying Roger was pleasantly exciting and most unattractive, and I glanced at his smooth hands with a kind of horror. His cheek to touch was always firm and taut like a child's, and his teeth were very clean and even. We drank our coffee in silence, and I watched all the people at the other tables: to me, sober and slightly sick, they all looked disgusting as they sank heavily into their chairs over plates of food that would have kept a child alive for a week. No wonder, I thought, that waiters always dislike their clients so much, when they see them at such sordid moments. I had myself taken a particular dislike to the couple at the next table, both fat Americans, both bulging from their ill-chosen clothes: she had been making a nuisance of herself throughout the meal, sending things back, changing her order, asking for things that weren't on the menu. She had started off with melon and had choked on the ginger, which she had applied with ludicrous liberality. From their highly intermittent conversation, I gathered that they spent their time eating all over Europe. I thought of the woman in the doctor's, who had been of the same build, though for different reasons.

They started on their coffee just as we were finishing ours. I watched her pour it out, with her fat dimpled beringed hands, and then I watched her reach for the sugar, except it wasn't the sugar, it was the ginger, which was in a small glass dish and which had been on their table throughout the meal. I knew it was the ginger; my attention had been drawn to it by the choking episode. Anyway, it was too fine for brown sugar and rather too pale. Fascinated, I watched her take a spoonful and stir it into her cup. It didn't quite mix and I was afraid that she was going to notice in time, but she didn't. She didn't take a drink for quite a while, but when she did she really gulped it down. I watched her face closely: her expression changed, her eyes twitched, and she put the cup down rather quickly. But she said nothing. She must have noticed, but she said nothing. In fact she finished the cup. I have never made up my mind whether she was too drunk to know what she had done or had too bad a palate; or whether she knew quite well but wasn't going to admit her error. Only waiters err.

Roger drove me home, as ever. We parted in the car in the road outside: it was not necessary to make any formal move towards discontinuing our contact because I knew quite well that Roger would not ring or try to see me again. He said that if I wanted help of any sort I was to get in touch with him, but I wouldn't want help, would I, he said. No, I agreed. Will you announce it in *The Times*, he asked, and I said certainly, why not: but thinking such announcements a waste of money, myself.

So much for Joe and Roger. I was of course acquainted with a few other people but most of them were neither here nor there. The only people that really worried me were my pupils. I never saw any of my superiors in the academic world and as far as I knew there was nothing in any of my endowments or scholarships about illegitimate children: there was some qualification in one of them about not being married, but I considered myself clear on that score. I saw no reason why my proposed career of thesis, assistant lectureship, lectureship and so on should be interrupted: I saw a few non-reasons, I must admit, but in my wiser moments I knew they would not weigh heavily enough against my talents. However, I was worried about the people I was teaching. They were an odd lot and I had taken them on for odd reasons. Most of my research student acquaintances who were not teaching regularly did a little private teaching, mostly for the money, and partly for the practice. At this time I was myself teaching four separate people for an hour a week, which involved about as much homework as I could find time for; I had foolishly consented to teach a wide and abstruse variety of subjects instead of sticking to my own field. My reasons for undertaking this work cannot have been financial, for I undercharged all of them, as I seriously distrusted the value of the commodity I was offering: somebody pointed out to me that as a good socialist I was making a grievous error by lowering the price of my profession which, God knows, was low enough anyway, and she was quite right too, but by then it was too late and I was humanly incapable of raising, once stated, my charges.

As a matter of fact, while distrusting the value of my own teaching, I felt a simultaneous pride and confidence in it because I knew quite well that I was offering this strange quartet a far higher standard of information and intelligence than they would have been likely to get elsewhere, particularly through the education agency that had sent them to me. Yet while I was expounding to them my theories, I was always overcome by a sense of inadequacy, for which I paid at a rate of seven and six an hour.

I suppose I taught because of my social conscience. I was continually aware that my life was too pleasant by half, spent as it was in the gratification of my own curiosity and of my peculiar aesthetic appetite. I have nothing against original research into minor authors, but I am my parents' daughter, struggle against it though I may, and I was born with the notion that one ought to do something, preferably something unpleasant, for others. So I taught. The identity of my pupils would certainly bear out this interpretation of my conduct, for they were as I have said an odd lot, and three of them at least would have been rejected by my more serious friends as a waste of time. The fourth was an orthodox enough case; a seventeen-year-old girl who had left boarding school under a cloud, and wanted coaching for her University Entrance. She was very bright, and easy to teach; in fact, she had been passed on to me by a reputable don and did not come from the same dubious source as the others.

The other three were a little difficult. One was an Indian, one a Greek, and one a Methodist minister. The first two were both hoping, quite vainly I thought, to get into university, and the Methodist minister just wanted to brush up his English literature by taking it at advanced level. The Indian, I regret to say, was really a dead loss, as I knew from the moment I set eyes on him: he was over thirty, I am sure, and had gold teeth and a dark brown suit. It was my initial despair at the sight of him, coupled with his insistence, that made me take him on, for I could not bear the thought that I might be mistaken. He arrived one morning to discuss the possibility of taking lessons, and I tried to ask him sensible questions about when he hoped to take his entrance examinations, and which college he hoped to apply for, and what was his experience of English literature; he replied with a pathetically confused and garbled account of his past career, full of references to Bombay University, which meant less than nothing to me, and then went on to say that he hoped to go to Jesus Christ's College at Cambridge, because that famous poet Wordsworth had been there. Oddly enough, I happened to know that Wordsworth had been at John's. I wished I had not known, for the awareness rattled me. Then I said what English literature had he studied, and he said that famous poet Harrison, or so I thought, until I realized that he must have said Henryson. I hastily made it quite clear that I knew nothing about Henryson at all, and that he had better find someone who knew more about the period than I did. Whereat he said plaintively that he had tried everyone else, and I thought yes, I bet you have. Even so, I managed for almost the first time in my life to say No, but he kept ringing me up, and in the end I thought I must give him the benefit of the doubt. After all, he had heard of Henryson, which was clever in itself, and if he knew anything about Henryson, then he would know more about him than me. And, who knows, all that rigmarole about Bombay University might have been true, and many a gold tooth shines above a heart of gold, and so on: so I took him on. It was a mistake. It was a useless task: we ploughed through the entrance syllabus and I actually organized him sufficiently to make him write off to Bursars for entrance papers, but he had no more hope of getting in than a child of ten. I could not decide whether it would be good for him to fail his exams and come to terms with reality, or whether it would have been better for him to have lived on forever convinced that he could have made it if only he could have found a tutor. Not that that could have been my decision anyway: the choice was not mine. But I did my best and I felt he was my responsibility.

The Greek was a very different case. He was a young lad called Spiro who also wanted to get into Oxford or Cambridge: he was only eighteen which, for a start, put his chances higher than the Indian's. He clearly came from an affluent family which he seemed to have mislaid somewhere on the Continent; one parent was usually in Rome and the other in Spain, though they shifted from time to time. I started on him about three weeks after I started on the Indian, and was expecting like despair, but he quickly convinced me that he had at least a superficial brightness and intelligence. His English was excellent, which helped. It was months, however, before I realized the truth about him. It is alarming to see how strong one's prejudices are and how convinced one is (or I am) that no foreigner can ever have quite the same standard of intelligence as products of the English educational system. I do not mean that I think foreigners are stupid; merely that I always doubt if they can do it on quite the same ground. But after a few weeks I realized that Spiro could. He was quite outstandingly gifted, so gifted that he could even beat the examination system and eighteen years of unhelpful inheritance. He had always told me what a fantastic prodigy he was, but the more he had said it the more I distrusted him, until with a little practice and very little guidance, he started to turn out weekly essays of the most excellent, orthodox practical criticism, which would have been a credit to any first-year scholar anywhere. I was amazed, delighted, and a little crestfallen to find how narrowly my judgment operated. I tried not to let him see how much my opinion of his chances had improved, but I knew he could tell. He was a shockingly self-confident, conceited boy, but he was only eighteen, and he had a right to be.

The Methodist minister was a quiet, diffident and charming man whose one anxiety was lest he should embarrass me by obtruding his religious opinions. He felt it his duty to do such set authors as Milton and T. S. Eliot, but his passion was for Wordsworth, whom he admired for all the reasons which I found most suspect. He would clearly pass A Level with ease, being much better read than most schoolboys, but his essays were not very well organized as he was out of practice, and knew little of critical vocabulary. Since he was only doing the course for pleasure and would get through the exams anyway, I just did not know whether I should press him about his weaknesses or not. I did not want to confuse his pleasure with technicalities, though that perhaps was precisely what he was paying me to do. So my corrections were always very tentative, as tentative as his references to God, which were bound to creep in on any discussion of Milton.

When the third month of my pregnancy drew to an end, I began to worry myself to death about these four dependants. My instinct was to tell them all I was ill and unable to continue the course, but I felt some guilt about doing this midway to the exams, when they would find it very difficult to get a replacement, and certainly not a replacement with anything like my cheapness or qualifications. One minute I would tell myself that it was none of their business if I had a baby or not, and the next I would be driven to tears by the sheer embarrassment and absurdity of the situation, which I did not think I had the stamina to bear. I knew that I would have to come to some decision, through the pressure of time and the growth of my belly; I had heard of people who had disguised their condition till six months or later, but I did not fancy such evasion. On the other hand, how could I possibly put the thing into words?

In the end the only one that I told was Spiro. I let the others draw their own conclusions. My schoolgirl, Sally Hitchins, certainly noticed, but did not dare to ask: she seemed rather admiring, and had indeed no right to be otherwise, in view of what she had let drop about her own stormy record and the reasons for her expulsion. The Indian did not see. He just did not notice or, if he did, it meant nothing to him. But for my Methodist minister I took to wearing a wedding ring; not a real wedding ring, needless to say, but the identical curtain ring which I had flashed round that disreputable hotel for Hamish so many years before. He was the only person for whom I ever stooped to such measures, and I tell myself that I did it for his sake and not for my own. I don't know what he thought of it: I suppose he must have concluded that I had contracted a hasty shotgun wedding as the wedding ring appeared so late in the proceedings, but perhaps he was too kind and Christian for such conjecture. A situation like mine certainly makes clear how little we know of each other's ignorances and illuminations.

I told Spiro, or rather one might say that Spiro told me. It was about a fortnight after my last evening with Roger. I was wearing a large grey man's sweater that I had had for years, over a skirt that I had let out with a piece of string; I did not look too bad, though obvious enough to the discerning eye, and Spiro was discerning enough. He had just arrived and I went into the kitchen to make us both a cup of coffee: I returned with the tray, which I put down on top of the bookcase while I went to pick up the little coffee table, intending to place it in a convenient position between our two seats, but Spiro dashed forward and wrenched the table from my grasp, saying, "No, no, no, you mustn't go carrying heavy things any more, allow me, allow me."

"Whatever do you mean?" I said, pulling the table firmly back from him: it weighed nothing anyway, being about two feet high and two feet square, and made of ugly canework, like a garden chair. I put the thing down where I had originally intended, then looked back at Spiro. But he was laughing. I knew that he knew and I was annoyed with him for laughing at me.

"There's nothing funny about it," I said crossly, and he pulled a ridiculous mock-serious face and said:

"No, no, I quite agree, I quite agree."

"Sit down," I said, "and read me your essay on Donne. If you ever wrote it."

"Certainly, certainly," he said, with a look of brazen complicit apology, and got his essay out of his briefcase and started to read it: it was very good but in reading it aloud he treated it with a certain mockery, as though he could equally well have written anything else on the subject. He was only eighteen and so sharp, as they say, that one day he would cut himself. I did not mind that he knew that I knew that he knew. He laughed, and did not feel sorry and offered to lift tables for me because he wished to provoke and not because he wished to display his sympathy. From him, too, my poverty must have been concealed.

When I went to see the doctor again, he said that he had managed to book me a bed in St. Andrew's Hospital which, as he expected me to know, was on Marylebone Road. From the way in which he told me, I could see that he expected gratitude and that he considered he had done more for me than might have been expected of him. I was duly grateful, though on what grounds I was not quite sure: later I thought of three possible reasons for his air of achievement. It was quite clever of him to have got me a bed at all, in view of the shortage of maternity beds, and very clever of him to have got me one so close, and in a teaching hospital with an excellent reputation. After telling me that he had made this booking, he then washed his hands of me with undisguised relief. "You can go to the clinic at the hospital," he said, "and they'll look after you there."

"Yes, of course," I said, as though I understood the whole procedure, though I wanted to ask him a dozen things, about when to go, and where to go, and whom to ask for: but he was a busy man and there was a long queue in the surgery outside, so I got up to leave.

"Thank you very much," I said for the tenth time, and set off to the door: but he called me back and said, "Now then, you don't want to go without your letter of introduction, do you?"

"Oh no, of course not," I said, as though it had just momentarily slipped my mind, and he handed over an envelope addressed to the Ante-Natal Clinic, St. Andrew's Hospital. It was a sealed envelope. I wondered what it said inside. I felt slightly better leaving with that in my pocket as at least I now knew the name of the clinic which I was expected to attend: in those days I was so innocent that I did not even know what a clinic was.

My first visit to that clinic was a memorable experience. I had ascertained the day and the time by telephone, a piece of forethought of which I felt moderately proud, and I duly presented myself on Wednesday afternoon. The hospital was easy enough to find, being a large sprawling building occupying a large area of ground on the north side of the Marylebone Road, not far from that elegant favourite of mine, Castrol House. St. Andrew's could not rival this latter building in architectural distinction; the central block appeared to be early eighteenth-century and had regularity if nothing else, but it was surrounded and overlapped and encroached upon by a hideous medley of neo-Gothic, nineteen-thirties, and nineteen-sixties excrescences, all of which had been added entirely at random, from the visual point of view at least. I was alarmed, not so much because the building was an eyesore, for my visual taste is very weak, but because I did not know how to get into it, nor which part to attack. There were innumerable doors and entrances, and I had a sense that the main door was certainly not the appropriate one. In the end, however, it was that one which I chose, as I thought there might at least be a reception desk inside it. Luckily, there was. I presented myself and my incriminating envelope and was told to go out again and find the Out Patients entrance, which the girl said was down a side street. So I went out and found the Out Patients and entered the building once more. Here, as I had suspected, there was no reception desk and no indication of any direction: there was a door marked HAEMOTOLOGY and a lot of dark gloss cream corridors. I stood there irresolute, feeling acutely ashamed at my own ignorance: it was an emotion that I had experienced often enough before, on my first day at school, for instance, or my first day at Cambridge, but then with some mixed pleasurable anticipation, and now with nothing for foreboding.

I was rescued from immobility by the arrival of another woman, very evidently pregnant, who came briskly through the doors from the street and set off with an air of speed and purpose down one of the cream corridors. I put two and two together, and followed her. Sure enough, she led me straight to the ante-natal clinic, which turned out to be a large hall with various small rooms leading off it, full of rows of chairs and waiting pregnant women. There was still five minutes to go before the clinic officially opened, for I had at least grown wise to the inevitable queueing, but the room was crowded already and there were only three or four chairs left. I occupied one of them and prepared to wait, and while I waited I had a good look at those who were waiting with me.

They had one thing in common, of course, though their conditions varied from the invisible to the grossly inflated. As at the doctor's, I was reduced almost to tears by the variety of human misery that presented itself. Perhaps I was in no mood for finding people cheering, attractive or encouraging, but the truth is that they looked to me an unbelievably depressed and miserable lot. One hears much, though mostly from the interested male, about the beauty of a woman with child, ships in full sail, and all that kind of metaphorical euphemism, and I suppose that from time to time on the faces of well-fed, well-bred young ladies I have seen a certain peaceful glow, but the weight of evidence is overwhelmingly on the other side. Anemia and exhaustion were written on most countenances: the clothes were dreadful, the legs swollen, the bodies heavy and unbalanced. There were a few cases of striking wear: a huge middle-aged woman, who could walk only with a stick, a pale thin creature with varicose veins and a two-year-old child in tow, and a black woman who sat there not with the peasant acceptance of physical life of which one hears, but with a look of wide-eyed dilating terror. She was moaning to herself softly, and muttering, almost as though she were already in labour: perhaps, like me, she was more frightened of the hospital than of anything else. Even those who had no evident complaints, and who might well have been expected to be full of conventional joy, were looking cross and tired, possibly at the prospect of such a tedious afternoon: there was a couple of young girls in the row in front of me, the kind of girls who chatter and giggle on buses and in cafés, but they were not giggling, they were complaining at great length about how their backs ached and how they felt sick and how they'd never get their figures back. It seemed a shame. And there we all were, and it struck me that I felt nothing in common with any of these people, that I disliked the look of them, that I felt a stranger and a foreigner there, and yet I was one of them, I was like that too, I was trapped in a human limit for the first time in my life, and I was going to have to learn how to live inside it.

After some time, various nurses arrived and things started to happen and the queue began to move. People disappeared, in a completely mystifying order, to have their blood pressure taken, and to be weighed, and to see Doctor This and Doctor That and the midwife. I sat there for a while wondering if anyone would come and ask me for my card, and when they didn't I decided I would have to find someone to give it to; eventually, afraid that I would be accused of queue-jumping, I rose tentatively to my feet and went in search of authority. I found a nurse who took my envelope and told me to go and sit down again, so I did, and prepared myself for an endless wait, but within a few minutes my name too was mysteriously called. "Mrs. Stacey," said the mechanical voice, "Mrs. Rosamund Stacey." I got up once more and found the nurse who had taken my letter. She turned to me and said,

What do you want? I said they'd just called my name out, what should I do? Go see the midwife, said the nurse. Where? I said, almost sharply, for I could see no possible reason why I or anyone else should be expected to know by instinct where midwives were. Oh, don't you know? she said, and pointed to a door leading off the hall in the far right-hand corner. I walked up to it, knocked and went in.

The midwife was a pretty lady with smart ginger hair and small features and blue eyes. "Hello, Mrs. Stacey," she said warmly, extending her hand from behind her desk, "I'm Sister Hammond, how do you do?"

"How do you do?" I said, thinking I had reached civilization at last, but feeling nonetheless impelled to continue, "but I'm not Mrs. Stacey, I'm Miss."

"Yes, yes," she smiled, coldly and sweetly, "but we call everyone Mrs. here. As a courtesy title, don't you think?"

She was a civilized lady and she could see that I was civilized, so I too smiled frostily, though I did not think much of the idea. We had some chat about how she didn't believe in natural childbirth, and the overcrowding of the maternity service, and then she made me fill in interminable forms and documents, giving details of all past illnesses and of my domestic accommodation. When I said that I had a flat with five rooms, kitchen and bathroom all to myself, her smile became even more courteous and cold: I could see that she saw me, and without wild inaccuracy, as one of these rich dissolute young girls about town, and I was rather relieved that her profession prevented her from inquiring why I had not done the sensible and expected thing and gone and had an expensive abortion. I did not like her, but I felt on safe ground with her, as I did not feel with all those bloated human people outside. Safe, chartered, professional, articulate ground.

When she had finished her interrogation, she said,

"Well, Mrs. Stacey, that's all for now, I'll be seeing you again in a month's time."

"Do you mean that's all for now?" I said, getting up with relief, but she said:

"Oh no, I'm afraid not altogether. I'm afraid you'll have to wait now to see Dr. Esmond."

"Oh, I see," I said. "I'm afraid I don't quite understand the routine here."

"Oh," she said, rising dismissively, all clean starch and coolness, "oh, you'll soon find your way around. People don't take long to find their way around."

So I went out and waited for Dr. Esmond, and I waited for him till the bitter end, when everyone else had gone. It was the first time that I had ever been examined, and I could have put up with Dr. Esmond, who was a grey-haired old man with rimless glasses, but I was not prepared for being examined by five medical students, one after the other. I lay there, my eyes shut, and quietly smiling to conceal my outrage, because I knew that these things must happen, and that doctors must be trained, and that medical students must pass examinations; and he asked them questions about the height of the fundus, and could they estimate the length of pregnancy, and what about the pelvis. They all said I had a narrow pelvis, and I lay there and listened to them and felt them, with no more protest than if I had been a corpse examined by budding pathologists for the cause of death. But I was not dead, I was alive twice over.

As Sister Hammond had prophesied, I got used to it. I learned what time to arrive and where to slip my attendance card in the pile so that I would get called early in the queue: they were so unsystematic that one could not really beat their system, but one could win occasionally on the odd point. I learned to read the notes upside down in the file that said Not to be Shown to the Patient. I learned how to present myself for inspection, with the minimum necessary clothes' removal. I learned that one had to bully them about iron pills and vitamin pills, because they would never remember. But it continued to be an ordeal, unillumined by even the most fitful gleams of comfort: my sole aim was to get out as quickly as possible. I hated most of all the chat about birth that went on so continually around me in the queue: everyone recounted their own past experiences, and those of their sisters and mothers and aunts and friends and grandmothers, and everyone else listened, spellbound, including me. The degrading truth was that there was no topic more fascinating to us in that condition; and indeed few topics anywhere, it seems. Birth, pain, fear and hope, these were the subjects that drew us together in gloomy awe, and so strong was the bond that even I, doubly, trebly outcast by my unmarried status, my education, and my class, even I was drawn in from time to time, and compelled to proffer some anecdote of my own, such as the choice story of my sister who gave birth to her second in an ambulance in a snow storm. Indeed, so strong became the pull of nature that by the end of the six months' attendance I felt more in common with the ladies at the clinic than with my own acquaintances.

Pregnancy revealed to me several interesting points, of which I had not before been aware. It was quite amazing, for instance, how many pregnant women there suddenly seemed to be in the world. The streets were crawling with them, and I never remembered having noticed them before. Even the British Museum, and I came to think most particularly the British Museum, was full of earnest intellectual women like myself, propping themselves or their unborn babies against the desk as they worked. The same discovery was to be made later with the babies. Also, I came to realize how totally I depended on the casual salute as my sole means of sexual gratification: now, of course, I was having to learn how to do without it, as men do not lean out of car windows to shout and whistle at expectant mothers, nor do they stare at them intently on tube trains, nor make pointed remarks about them in cafés or shops. In my time I had received much of this kind of attention, being tall and well-built and somehow noticeable, and it had given me much pleasure. The more tenuous a link, the more pleasure it would give me, as I could no longer fail to admit: after all, my affair with George must have been as tenuous as any contact likely to produce such a positive result could possibly have been. George, George, I thought of George, and sometimes I switched on the radio to listen to his voice announcing this and that: I still could not believe that I was going to get through it without telling him, but I could not see that I was going to tell him either. I would have the odd two minutes when I would think of him, and such grief and regret and love would pour down my spine that I tried not to think.

My acquaintances took it pretty much as one would have expected, with a mixture of curiosity, admiration, pity and indifference. There must have been some speculation as to whose the child was, but I did not know any group of people well enough to be asked to my face—except in the most frivolous, easy-to-parry terms. I tried to convey, without saying anything, that there was a man somewhere whom none of them knew anything about, and that everything was all right really. The only person, however, who was truly fascinated by the event was Lydia Reynolds, my novelist friend. I used to meet Lydia for lunch from time to time as she worked near the British Museum in an art gallery which specialized in water colours. She would sometimes come to the Museum, too, to type in the typing room, but had not been for some time, so I assumed her work was going badly. When she first learned of my condition, somewhere round the end of the fourth month, all she said was:

"It's not Joe's, is it? I hope to God it isn't Joe's. I can't think what a baby belonging to Joe would turn out like, and anyway he does quite enough propagation, doesn't he?"

I assured her that it wasn't Joe's and she seemed quite happy. I then asked her how her own creative life was coming along, and she scowled and looked down at the table and with her left eye starting its habitual violent neurotic twitch, said bitterly:

"Oh, quite quite frightful. I can't get anything to work, I get worse and worse, I've got nothing to say, I've just got nothing to say."

"If you've got nothing to say," I said, "why try to say it? Why not have a little rest?"

"I *can't* rest," she said violently, "I can't rest. When I'm not working on something I'm so miserable, I'm so unhappy, I don't exist, I can't do anything, I can't enjoy a thing."

"It'll pass," I said placating.

"I don't see why," she said. "Perhaps I'm finished."

"If you really thought you were, you wouldn't say so."

"Wouldn't I? Perhaps not. But what about people like Joe though, how do they keep at it, one a year, year in, year out? Where do they get it from?"

"I thought you didn't like Joe's work."

"I don't."

"Then why worry about it?"

"I can't help worrying. I'd rather write a bad book than nothing."

"Why don't you write one then?"

"I can't," she wailed. "I can't. I try to. I begin them but I can't finish. How I envy you, Rosamund, your work is always there, you know what's got to be done, it's all there outside you waiting for you to come and straighten it out and put it together, like a job almost, like a job to be done. I wish I could write a book on something and not just a book. I wish I didn't have to go on dragging it out of myself like a dirty great spider. I wish I could write a book on Elizabethan poets."

"There's nothing to stop you," I said, but she sighed heavily and said, chewing savagely at the quick of her nails:

"Ah, there, I haven't got your education."

The next time I saw her she told me all about her miscarriage. She started off by saying that she thought I must be crazy to be having the baby, ruining my life, and all the old junk, but she did not mean it seriously, she was merely leading in to what she herself had to say. "I suppose the truth is," she concluded, "that you must really want it. On some level, don't you think?"

I shrugged my shoulders, for I did not know the answer. Then she went on:

"It's a funny thing, you know," she said, "but I was pregnant once. It was awful. It was just after the first novel was published, and I came down to London for the first time and I got mixed up with a whole crowd of idiots and slept about all over the place. It was great fun, especially after Doncaster, but I was such a fool in those days, I knew all about everything in theory but practice was another matter and, anyway, after a while I realized what was up. I was determined not to have it, but on the other hand I couldn't bear the thought of having anything scruffy done, being so neurotic and all that I thought it might upset me, so I got this fellow to recommend me this really expensive chap who did everything legally, on psychological grounds and so on, you know what I mean, private nursing home, all that lark. So I made myself an appointment and off I went to convince this man that if I had this baby I was going to be a mental and physical wreck, which is the wording of that case, you know the one I mean. He was an old fat man and quite nice. He lived on the Bayswater Road. Anyway, he asked me all my life story and I told him the whole lot, which was great fun—ferocious mother, dad bumped himself off because she bullied him, four-roomed house, squalor, sent to work at sixteen, the whole lot, and I made it sound as lurid as I could, and the whole time I made myself look as neurotic as I possibly could, which was easy enough with the material I've got. By the end of my recital I felt so sorry for myself I nearly burst into tears. He too seemed moved, and I thought I was well away, but when I finished he said he was very sorry but in my case he was afraid that he couldn't possibly recommend termination of the pregnancy. He said I was too sensitive and impressionable and conscientious, and that in cases like mine termination was far more likely to lead to a breakdown than going to full term. I tried to explain that I certainly wouldn't have a breakdown anyway, and he said that if I wasn't going to have a breakdown anyway then what was I there for. There didn't seem to be any way out of it: he would only recommend termination for people who were so insensitive that they wouldn't break down because of it, yet presumably if they were so insensitive then they wouldn't be going to see him in the first place. The whole thing was a real waste of time, he was quite the wrong kind of person altogether; I don't know where this chap got him from. In the end I didn't know whether to try to persuade him that I was perfectly well-balanced and totally indifferent to all the moral issues, or whether I ought to convince him that I was so far over the edge that he had to rescue me before too late."

"What on earth did you do?" I asked, feeling some relief that I had not tried this confusing course myself.

"Oh, in the end I walked out, I could see we weren't getting anywhere. He was the wrong kind of man; he was some perfectly serious psychiatrist who had happened to write some article on Abortion Law Reform, and this chap of mine who recommended him had got hold of the wrong end of the stick."

"So what did you do?"

"Well, this is the funny bit. I walked out, and I was feeling rather indignant and wrapped up in my own thoughts and what I should do, and would I have to go to some awful butcher, and how I was going to give Lawrence hell when I got hold of him, and the long and the short of it is that I was so upset that I walked straight across the Bayswater Road and got knocked down by a bus. I wasn't really hurt, but the fright did the trick and without any effort at all on my part. Right outside his front door too. I'd swear he was watching from his window when the ambulance came and picked me up."

"What a stroke of luck," I said.

"Yes, it was, wasn't it? And nobody ever suggested that I'd done it on purpose because it wasn't the kind of accident that one could possibly plan, I mean one would have been more likely to be killed than to miscarry. I really felt providence was on my side. It was the most extraordinary thing that ever happened to me, I think."

"Why don't you put it in a book?" I said. "That would give you something to write about."

"Oh, I couldn't possibly," said Lydia. "It's so unconvincing. Far too unrealistic for my kind of novel. It sounds like something out of Hardy's *Life's Little Ironies*."

"I've always thought *Life's Little Ironies* had rather a profound attitude to life," I said truthfully.

"Have you really?" said Lydia. "I don't find it profound at all. It's so mechanical. Not real."

"But it was real. It happened to you."

"Ah yes," said Lydia, "but there's a difference between what happens to one in real life and what one can make real in art. That happened to me, I agree it happened to me, but I'm not convinced by it, it hasn't got the kind of stamp of reality on it to me. I don't write about that kind of thing, I couldn't. And anyway I don't like accidents in books. Who was it who said: The moving accident is not my trade? It's not mine either."

"Wordsworth."

"Was it really? I didn't know I knew any Wordsworth."

"So you don't think that because something happens, that makes it true?" I said.

"No, not at all," said Lydia. "Do you?"

"I suppose I must," I said.

In bed that night I thought for some time about life's little ironies, for the truth was, as I had told Lydia, that they always moved me out of all proportion to their significance in any respectable philosophic scheme. I have always been stirred, sometimes profoundly, by newspaper comments such as Killed While Adjusting Safety Belt, or Collapsed Night Before Wedding. I used to think that my interest in such cases sprang from some absurd belief in a malicious deity: but now, lying there in bed with my hands folded over my stirring, unknown baby, it occurred to me that my interest had been a premonition of a different, non-rational order of things. My present predicament would certainly qualify, I thought, as one of life's little ironies, and yet it did not seem to be a mere accident, nor the effect of divine malevolence. Had it belonged to the realm of mere accident I would have surely got rid of it, for though I am a coward about operations and hospitals, even then I could see that I was letting myself in for more hospitals and more unpleasantness by continuing than I would have done by termination. But it did not seem the kind of thing one could have removed, like a wart or a corn. It seemed to have meaning. It seemed to be the kind of event to which, however accidental its cause, one could not say No.

At the same time it did not seem to be totally the product of malevolence. I did not feel, as Hardy felt for Tess, that events had conspired maliciously against my innocence. Perhaps I did not wish to feel this, for it was a view dangerous to my dignity and difficult to live with for the years which were to come. The more I thought about it, the more convinced I became that my state must have some meaning, that it must, however haphazard and un-expected and unasked, be connected to some sequence, to some significant development of my life. These were the things I thought before the child was born, of course, for a child once born is significant enough in itself: but the point is that before the birth I did not know this and was puzzled as by hints and warnings of what was to be. My state was curious; it was as though I were waiting for some link to be revealed to me that would make sense of discon-nections, though I had no evidence at all that it existed. At times I had a vague and complicated sense that this preg-nancy had been sent to me in order to reveal to me a scheme of things totally different from the scheme which I inhabited, totally removed from academic enthusiasms, social consciousness, etiolated undefined emotional con-nections, and the exercise of free will. It was as though for too long I had been living in one way, on one plane, and the way I had ignored had been forced thus abruptly and violently to assert itself. Really, it was a question of free will; up to this point in my life I had always had the illusion at least of choice, and now for the first time I seemed to become aware of the operation of forces not totally explicable, and not therefore necessarily blinder, smaller, less kind or more ignorant than myself.

These were forces which I had always derided when they had been mentioned in conversation by others; irrational self-justification, I had called them. They had always been dragged up in connection with such dicy topics as marriage and maternity, in which luck or blind chance play a large part. My sister in particular had been particularly prone to comments of this nature. All three of her pregnancies had been accidental, as the saying is, and she had commented thus: "You don't decide to have children. They decide to be born."

She had also made several ludicrous remarks of a less portentous nature, while expecting her third child, all of which seemed to spring from this hinterland of unwilled consequences and confused values.

"Honestly," she said once, and with sincerity, not flippancy, "I'm delighted about this, now I'll be able to use up all my baby clothes. I've got so many, I was dreading having to pack them up to send them to Oxfam, I so hate making parcels."

And at some other juncture she had said to me, "Do you know, at least a week before I could possibly have *known* about this baby, I went into Marks for some new underwear and *quite by accident* bought myself a couple of pairs of WX pants that had got mixed up on the ordinary counter, and when I got them home I actually *said* to myself, these would come in handy if ever I were pregnant again, which of course I had no intention of being, even though I actually *was*." These things seemed to weigh as nothing in the balance compared with the life of a child, nor could I imagine to myself in cold blood a diety however obscure rearranging the underwear in a department store; yet, I began to see, somehow, what she had meant.

I do not wish to suggest, as perhaps I seem to be suggesting, that the irrational was taking its famed feminine grip upon me. My Elizabethan poets did not begin to pale into insignificance in comparison with the thought of buying nappies. On the contrary, I found I was working extremely well at this time and with great concentration and clarity. I thought continually and with relief that I was as sure about the Elizabethan poets as I was sure that I liked baked potatoes. I did not go over from the camp of logic to the camp of intuition; it was rather that I became aware of the facts that I had not recognized or even noticed before. There is nothing logical about ignorance. I am sure that my discoveries were common discoveries; if they were not, they would not be worth recording. The only curious feature in my case is that the facts that I now discovered were precisely the same facts that my admirable parents had always so firmly presented to our childish eyes: facts of inequality, of limitation, of separation, of the impossible, heartbreaking uneven hardship of the human lot. I had always felt for others in theory and pitied the blows of fate and circumstance under which they suffered; but now, myself no longer free, myself suffering, I may say that I felt it in my heart.

Hitherto in my life I had most successfully avoided the bond that links man to man, though I had paid it some lip service; the closest and most serious connections I had ever known had been with people like Joe, Roger, and indeed George, connections which seem trivial enough to recount but upon which I had expended a good deal of attention as idle, refined, educated single girls will: and, fool that I was, I thought that this was what life was about. I was never fool enough to think that one can get something for nothing; I knew one had to pay one's way and I considered that I had paid mine by the wit of my conversation, by a certain inherited prestige, by having a nice flat for parties, and by possessing a fine pair of legs. These things were as nothing compared with the bonds that bind parent and child, husband and wife, child and aged parent, where money and responsibility are all that count, but I did not find that out until much later. However, it did occur to me one day, quite early on, that although I recognized the principle of payment, I had some basic deficiency when it came to taking appropriate goods in exchange.

It occurred to me one day in the clinic, when I was five months gone, and feeling rather well, as one does at that stage. I was sitting patiently waiting, having arrived unavoidably late, and was leafing through Rosamund Tuve, when somebody came and sat down on the chair next to me. The chair groaned under her weight, but I did not look up immediately, having reached an interesting point about George Herbert: after a minute or so, however, I became aware that a small child was standing on my foot, so I looked at it, ready to make disapproving shufflings. It was a small boy, about two, wearing corduroy trousers of considerable dirty shabbiness, a brown jacket, and a grey knitted balaclava helmet. He looked tired and pathetic and I glanced at his mother with curiosity. She was a large, short woman with dark hair and an old green coat, and there was a foreignness in her features: she could have been Italian, or half-Italian, and her face had an expressionless, solid immobility as though none of it would or could move. On her knee was a baby, asleep: it was large and fat, and looked about nine months old or so to my inexpert eyes. She never looked at the little boy at all: when I had dislodged him from my feet, he wandered off to the other end of the room and started climbing on the empty chairs, trying the door handles of the changing cubicles, and kicking the radiators, with a face as expressionless as his mother's. She just stared straight ahead and the word that was written on her was endurance.

After a while, the nurse came and called her name. "Mrs. Sullivan," she called in her thin shallow voice, and the woman next to me stirred and responded, but did not get up: she looked around her for the boy and then looked at me and said, in a flat tone, "Would you hold the little one for me? It doesn't seem fair, like, to wake him up, and he plays up something shocking if he doesn't have his sleep out. Would you have him for a few ticks for me, duck?"

I could not have said No, though I was afraid of my charge, and she handed over to me the large and sleeping infant, and rose to her feet: I saw with alarm that she must be at least six months pregnant, even allowing for natural lapse of the figure through two successive births. She made her way off to the midwife's room and I sat there with this huge and monstrously heavy child sitting warm and limp upon my knee, his nose slightly running and his mouth open to breathe. I was amazed by his weight; my legs felt quite crushed under it. I also realized that he was not only warm but damp; his knitted leggings were leaking quite copiously onto my knee. I shifted him around but did not dare to move much for fear of waking him and having to put up with his playing up something shocking: I was worried about whether the damp patch would show on my coat, and hoped it would not. I sat there for a good ten minutes with this child upon my lap; it was the first time I had ever held a baby and after a while, simultaneously with preoccupations about damp on my coat, a sense of the infant crept through me, its small warmness, its wide soft cheeks, and above all its quiet, snuffly breathing. I held it tighter and closed my arms around it.

Before its mother and brother returned, however, my name too was called: I was due to see the gynecologist that week, not the midwife. "Mrs. Stacey," the nurse called, and then again, "Mrs. Stacey," and there I was, trapped there with this child upon my knee, afraid to move, afraid to miss my turn, afraid of annoying the nurse. I could not pass the child along the row like a parcel: I was beginning to panic when the woman re-emerged from the midwife's office and I was able to return her child without too much delay.

The gynecologist did not keep me long: apparently I was the most normal of cases, not worth the attention of his students. I left as ever with relief, and started off, tolerably light of foot, along the Marylebone Road towards Ulster Place, where I was going to have tea with some old college friends. On the way, only a couple of blocks along, I overtook the woman with her two children. She was going painfully slowly along the other side of the road: the elder child was stopping to look in every litter bin and to run up the steps of every building, and she did not hurry him along but paused to wait for him, hardly looking at what he was doing but standing still, eyes fixed, the smaller child slung, legs astride, over the swelling of the next. There was a solemnity about her imperceptible progress that impressed me deeply: she stood there, patiently waiting, like a warning, like a portent, like a figure from another world. Five months earlier I would have passed her without another glance, but now the weight of her child was heavy in my arms and my coat still damp from his dampness. I do not know how she could get along that road. Nor could I feel that weight till my own arms had tested it.

When I reached my friends, I thought I might tell them about the child and how I had held it, so that I could laugh it away; they were nice girls, three of them sharing a flat, one now an actress, one a civil servant, and one like me doing research, and at Cambridge we had recounted for a laugh our most intimate defeats. I started off now on the woman in green, and they began to listen with a tender interest: but I could not be bothered to tell them because as soon as I started to speak I realized that I had not taken it in, I had not got it into a state fit for anecdote, as Lydia had not arranged her miscarriage sufficiently for fiction. I did not find out what it had meant to me until after the birth of my own child: though part of it I made out sooner, as I left their flat for home. I saw that from now on I, like that woman, was going to have to ask for help, and from strangers too: I who could not even ask for love or friendship.

As I walked home, I thought seriously for the first time about what I was going to do, with a child in my arms and work to do. So averse was I to help of any kind that I could not put up with any form of domestic assistance: I could not pay anyone to do dirty work that I could do myself. I had my upbringing to thank for this attitude, though I know it is not technically good socialism, and my parents themselves were not so ludicrously obstinate about such details; but it has always been my fault to be too scrupulous. It is not virtue, it is not morality: by my scruples I was denying some woman four bob an hour for as many hours as it would have taken to rescue that large flat from the squalor into which it was forever threatening to sink. With a baby, though, I could not afford such scruples. Also, I would have to go to the library to work, and one cannot take babies to libraries. Something would have to be done, plans would have to be made. I could feel that my own personal morality was threatened: I was going to have to do things that I couldn't do. Not things that were wrong, nothing as dramatic as that, but things that were against the grain of my nature.

When I got home, I sat down with *The Times,* and started to go through the Domestic Advertisements. I was bewildered by the social connotations of phrases like Mother's Help, Au Pair girl, Nanny, Housekeeper. It seemed that I neither wanted nor could afford any of these things: I made myself look at the problem and was just concluding that the most and least I could put up with would be a child minder for so many hours per day per week, when the doorbell rang. I got up to answer it: sometimes, from the unease with which I rose to answer such unexpected calls, I would wonder if I had so thoroughly abandoned all expectation of ever seeing George again. Occasionally, even now, I would picture to myself scenes in which he would arrive on my doorstep and greet me with phrases like "Rosamund, I've tried to live without you and I can't" or "Rosamund, I've loved you ever since I set eyes on you": occasionally, with shame, I would go through the whole romantic paraphernalia of meetings at the ends of long corridors, of embraces at the top of wide staircases, of passionate encounters at Oxford Circus. I would tell myself in reproof that these images were born of fear, not love, and so they doubtlcss were. Anyway, when I answered the door this time it was Lydia Reynolds.

"I *am* sorry to trouble you," she said, when I let her in,

"but I've just had a series of minor disasters and the long and the short of it is that I've got to ask you if you can put me up for the night. You will say no, won't you, if it's not convenient?"

"It's perfectly convenient," I said as we went and sat down in the sitting room. "Tell me about the disasters."

"I couldn't possibly refrain from telling you about the disasters," said Lydia, and launched into them forthwith. It seemed that the girl whose flat she had been sharing had been rejoined by her husband, who had been absent for some months, and had reclaimed his right to residence: the wife had been reluctant to part with Lydia and her rent, as she placed no reliance on her husband's permanence in the ménage, so for a few days they had all struggled along together, in two rooms and a kitchen, with Lydia sleeping on the settee. The husband had then become irritated by Lydia's continual presence and had told her to get out, whereupon the wife had burst into tears over the breakfast table and had said that she preferred Lydia to him, and she wished he would get out instead. Lydia had realized that she should have left at this point, in order not to confuse other people's matrimonial problems, "but," she said, "I just couldn't face the thought of finding myself a new place and moving all my stuff out, especially when anyone could see they wouldn't last the month, so I hung on and I'd have stuck it out only last night I got in very late and was undressing very quietly and considerately when the wretched man emerged from the bathroom and made a grab at me, so after that I felt I was *non grata* on all counts, so I left this morning."

"Well," I said, "you might as well stay here until he leaves."

"Perhaps he won't leave," said Lydia. "Just to spite me after what I said to him last night. The awful thing was that he was rather attractive. The only justification for his existence, I expect. I used to like out-and-out bastards like that, but I've right gone off them recently. Give me nice timid decent little men like Alex; they're the kind I really get on with."

"Does she like him?"

"I suppose she must. Or must have done. I'm not so sure that she hasn't gone off him too. And there's another thing. I lost my job this week."

"Oh dear," I said mildly. "Why?"

"I kept on not going," said Lydia plaintively, "and in the end they said I'd not gone once too often. I don't blame them either. But the result of all this is that I'm broke."

"Oh," I said, "perhaps I could lend you . . ."

"Oh no," she said, "nothing like that. I've got a bit here and there, it was just that I was going to ask you a favour and since you suggested it yourself, I mean to say it's not as though . . . anyway, what about my moving in with you? I could baby-sit for you and all that. I'd pay you rent of course, but it'd have to be fairly nominal, you know what I mean. I'd be very useful to you, don't you think? I could pick things up for you, and carry your shopping basket. That is, if it's not too much trouble. I mean, you haven't got anyone else living here, have you?"

Clearly she was referring to my prospective child's elusive father: I shook my head and denied any other lodgers. The more I thought about the scheme, the more hopeful it seemed, because there was plenty of room, and the thought of having to ring alone for the ambulance had begun to haunt me slightly: though the greatest point in its favour was that she had suggested it as a favour to herself and that I had not had to ask. To put myself totally in the clear and upper position, I insisted that she should pay no rent, explaining that as I paid none myself, and as my parents had let me have the flat so that none should be paid, I could not dream of taking anything off her, though we could split the electricity bills. She heaved a sigh of relief and seemed genuinely elated by the prospect.

"It's so *posh* round here," she said, "and you're so posh, and I do have such a thing about being posh."

"I bet you move out," I said, "when the baby arrives. Babies aren't posh at all, you know."

"Rubbish," she said, "I agree that ordinary babies aren't much of a status symbol, but illegitimate ones are just about the last word."

We celebrated our agreement with the remains of a bottle of very sour wine and some bacon and eggs, then Lydia rang up all her friends to tell them where she was, which precipitated some discussion about the phone bill. Then she said where was the television, and I said I didn't have a television and would on no account have one in the house, I had too much work to do. She didn't think much of that and asked if she could borrow a nightie, she wanted to go to bed. So I found her a nightie and we made up the bed, and then we had a long discussion about Joe Hurt, whom Lydia had seen the week before. Eventually we stopped talking and I too went to bed, where I fell asleep more happily than I had done for months, relieved, and without any of the weakness of intervention, of the oppressive loneliness that had been worrying me for some time. I liked Lydia: she was intelligent and self-reliant and interesting, and she had wanted of her own accord to come and live with me. The following week she acquired a rented television, which I made her put in her bedroom and I would go and sit on her bed with her and watch it: she had started another novel and would type noisely through all the programs, so I made her move it back into the sitting room but then she came and typed in the sitting room because, she said, the noise of the machine helped her to concentrate.

Housekeeping with Lydia worked quite well and after a fortnight of it I felt I should make other steps towards setting my house in order. I had been intending for some time to write and tell my sister of the situation: I did not mean to inform my brother at all, as he would have been heartily outraged by my behaviour, and as I have said it did not seem worth upsetting quite needlessly my parents. My sister, however, I was sure would be sympathetic, as she had always sung to me the praises of motherhood and domesticity: I used to accuse her of the reverse principle of sour grapes, of the desire to trap others in her own snare, by praising the pleasures of confinement, because there could be no doubt that she did suffer for her choice. Like me, she was very much our parents' daughter: educated to be independent and to consider herself the equal of anyone alive, she had a streak of practical earnestness that reminded me very much of my mother. She, too, had been to university, though to Oxford, not Cambridge, and she had moved in slightly more solidly intellectual and committed circles than I had ever discovered. She had met there her future husband, a scientist called Hallam who had then been a junior fellow: she herself read economics, so they had some meeting ground. They got married shortly after she came down, whereupon Hallam promptly took up a job on an atomic research station and carried her off to a deserted spot in the Midlands populated only by other atomic scientists, their wives, tradesmen and engineers. Beatrice had immediately had three children and made a virtue of necessity: but I often felt that she suffered strongly from a graduate sense that she was not using her degree to its best advantage. Her conscience was doubtless appeased by the unpleasantness of her social life and the rigour of rearing three small children: it was not, after all, as though she had got out of economics in order to idle her life away at the hairdresser's.

Ideologically, poor Beatrice was in an unfortunate position: unlike any of the rest of the family, she was a confirmed pacifist, or had been at Oxford. She must have found living on an atomic research station extremely trying: Hallam luckily shared her political views and assured her continually that knowledge was the only way to safety, and that he was thus furthering, to the best of his ability, the cause of world peace. He may have been right, though that was clearly not his motive for doing his work. Having swallowed this, Beatrice began to take the line of realistic compromise all along, and to frown slightly on our parents' singleness of mind. The question of pacifism still preyed on her mind, however: she wrote to me once and told me that their oldest boy, Nicholas, had reached the violent age, and was forever playing at guns, soldiers, cowboys, and, worst of all, bombs. "Whenever I tell him to finish his pudding," she wrote plaintively, "he turns on me and makes a horrible noise and says 'Bang, you're dead.' " One day, enraged beyond endurance by this inevitable and infuriating response, she had clouted him hard on the side of his head: "which," she said, "is *completely* against my principles, and anyway makes complete nonsense of the principle of passive resistance, don't you think? It was like a world war in miniature, if you know what I mean." The wretched child claimed that he had developed earache as a result of her unprecedented attack and she had suffered torments of remorse until it cleared up and proved to be nothing at all, just spite.

Anyway, when I wrote and told Beatrice about the baby, it was with every expectation of receiving goodwill and sympathy by return of post: and I was looking forward to it, for I felt I had lived without sympathy for long enough. I was quite proud of the way that I had managed, and I might even have expected some kind of congratulations upon my restraint. The letter that I received, however, was this.

My dear Rosamund,

I can't tell you how worried and upset we were by your news. I am quite amazed that you didn't let us know earlier; from what you say I gather that the baby is due in four months. I do think you should have let us know. You say not to tell the parents, but you must know they are bound to find out sooner or later, and surely you can't intend to go on living in the flat without letting them know. Obviously they'll be very upset but you know what they're like, they would never hold anything against you—since you say not to tell them, of course I won't, but I do wish you would. And what about Andrew? I know you never see him and I don't blame you, but what if you were to run into him or something, or if any of his friends were to see you in the street? It would be awful if they heard through him because he wouldn't think twice.

Don't think I'm not sympathetic, I am; I think it's quite frightful for you, I don't know how you can stick it. I'm glad your work isn't suffering, anyway.

I must say you didn't go into many details about the whole thing, but from what you said I gathered you were intending to keep the child. I feel I must tell you that I think this is the most dreadful mistake, and would be frightful for both you and the child—just think, if you had it adopted you could forget about the whole business in six months and carry on exactly where you left off. That would be much better for you, don't you think? You can have no conception of what it means to have a child, of the responsibility and the worries and the financial anxiety and the not being able to get out or do anything without planning. Believe me, I know. I just can't see you adapting yourself to the demands it would make on you, you've always been so set on your independence and having your own way. You can have no idea of what it means to have to think of someone else, twenty-four hours of every day, and not for a year or two but for ever, more or less. However, it isn't just you that I'm thinking of. It would be bad enough for you but it would be far, far worse for the child. Through no fault of its own it would have to have the slur of illegitimacy all its life, and I can't tell you how odiously cruel and vicious children can be to each other, once they get hold of something like that. A baby isn't just something you can have just because you feel you ought. Because you oughtn't, and that's that. It's your duty to have it adopted by some couple who really want a child, and who are probably in a far more favourable position for bringing one up. I know that ideally, in a decent society, no child ought to suffer because of this kind of handicap, but this isn't a decent society, and I can't bear the thought of what your baby would have to go through, and what you would have to go through on its account. Do please think about this and try to take a long term view. And if I can give you a piece of warning, when you decide to have it adopted, for God's sake don't let yourself see too much of it. You have to keep them for a certain amount of time, I think, don't you, but for God's sake don't let yourself get involved with it. It's a quite meaningless kind of involvement at that age and you'll be the only one to suffer. Another thing is that you don't even mention the father in your letter, so I assume he's somebody you don't want or can't associate yourself with, so presumably you wouldn't want to ask him for financial help, would you? If you do want some money, do let us know and we'll see what we can do. But think how frightful it would be to see the child of someone one didn't like growing up in one's home. It's bad enough when it's the child of someone you *do* like. Poor Rosamund, how absolutely rotten for you. I wish I could come and give you a hand, but I'm so tired at the moment, and they've all got frightful colds. It sounds a good hospital anyway, which is something. The whole business of being pushed around is quite horrid but one just has to grit one's teeth. Anyway, both of us send you all our love, and do keep in touch. And look after yourself, for goodness sake, don't rush around too much, will you.

Best love,
Beatrice

I read this letter, as can be imagined, with some dismay. I could see that she was writing out of genuinely strong concern but nevertheless I was indignant and annoyed. It seemed to me that nobody had the faintest right to offer me any advice about my own child: I had not asked for advice, I was quite capable of advising myself. Her letter did in fact serve one purpose: it revealed to me the depth of my determination to keep the baby. The determination at this stage cannot have been based, as it later was, on love, for I felt no love and little hope of feeling it: it was based rather on an extraordinary confidence in myself, in a conviction, quite irrational, that no adoptive parents could ever be as excellent as I myself would be. At the same time, the prospect of motherhood frightened me; I experienced the usual doubts about whether my child would like me, whether I would like my child, and so on, but simultaneously with these doubts I experienced absolute certainty. I knew for a fact that the child would be mine and that I would have it. Whatever Beatrice said, I would have felt it a cowardly betrayal to abandon it to the unknown, well-meaning ignorance of anyone else in Britain.

One result of her letter Beatrice cannot have foreseen. Her reference to living with the child of a man one did not like suggested to me for the first time the picture of a baby like George. I found the picture painfully vivid and felt a dangerous impulse to ring him up and tell him that instant: I did not, of course, but that evening I switched on the radio, a luxury I had not permitted myself for some time, and listened to his voice. He sounded so civil and so innocent that once more I could not imagine that I could ever have dreamed that I might encumber him with embarrassment and anxiety. I looked back once more over everything that he had ever said to me and I would have given a good deal if I could have heard him say, just once more, in his camp and gentle tone, "Well, well, my goodness me, Rosamund, and aren't we looking pretty this evening." Though we never did look at all pretty these days, we had to admit.

When I was young, I used to be so good-natured. I used to see the best in everyone, to excuse all faults, to put all malice and shortcoming down to environment: in short, to take all blame upon myself. But for the child, I might have gone on like that forever and, who knows, I might have been the better and nicer for it in the kindness of my innocence. I repeat; not being blind, I saw faults but I excused them. Now I felt less and less like finding excuses. I still cringed politely and smiled when doors slammed in my face, but I felt resentment in my heart. For instance, when I was five months pregnant, though not admittedly in my winter coat looking it, I was sitting in a tube train when two middle-aged women got on: there were no more seats so they stood in front of me, strap hanging, and proceeded to grumble, very pointedly, about the ill manners of the young. As I happened to be the youngest person in the compartment, I could not but take this personally. They clearly meant to be overheard, for they went on and on in refined, mean, grating tones: looking back, I can see that they were nuts, and sad ones at that, but what I felt as I listened to them was fury. I had been reared to stand for the elderly on public transport; and after a while I could bear it no longer, and I heaved myself to my feet and offered one of them my place. I made the gesture with extreme ill-feeling and indeed malice, but the woman took my seat without a word of thanks but with a tired, reproving pursing of the lips, and as I stood there it became clear that she did not notice my condition. It was the only time that I wished I were as huge as a house as some women are: though in fact size is meaningless, as one feels worst in the first three months when nothing is on view. I stood there and watched her sitting, and I was full of hate. I wanted to faint on the floor, to show her. But then, who knows, she must have had her afflictions too.

For my brother and his wife, too, I used to make excuses: I used to try to see them in perspective and to regard not them but what had made them what they were. I suppose I felt ashamed of an emotion as irrational as dislike. I did not see them very often: dutifully, perhaps, twice a year. I had thought they would be easy enough to avoid; unlike Beatrice, I had no fears that I would meet them idly in the street. But then, of course, I went and did precisely that: I met her, anyway. I was in Selfridge's Food Market, buying a bag of wholemeal flour, as Lydia and I were in the middle of a highly temporary craze for baking our own bread, and there she was, staring earnestly at the delicious rows of stuffed and larded game birds, no doubt shopping for one of her excruciating dinners. When I saw her, I instantly turned and started to walk away but she must have looked up at the same moment, for I heard her call, in piercing Kensington tones, "Rosamund, Rosamund." I turned and walked slowly back towards her and her eyes took in my state.

"Hello, Clare," I said when I reached her. "Buying a pheasant or two, then?"

She looked slightly confused, as well she might, and muttered, playing for time, "I was just buying a few things for dinner tomorrow." She was wearing a dusky pink coat with a fur collar and a hat that made her look twice her age: she cannot be more than twenty-eight and she looks a good forty at times. A good young forty, well-preserved by care and protection from the weather. She is neither pretty nor plain, and she has a mania for cleanliness: on one of our first meetings, when she still thought we might be good friends, she was telling me how many times she had her clothes cleaned. "If there's one thing I can't *stand*," she said with a violent shudder, "it's dirty clothes. Don't you agree?" The remark had astonished me, as I had hardly spared the question a thought till that moment, and certainly could not summon up any violence to support her; I had just said "Oh yes, I suppose so," while glancing surreptitiously at the state of my own long unwashed jersey. Since then we had abandoned all pretense at common ground, apart from family matters. I suppose poor Clare had an intellectual inferiority complex; she should have done if she had not, as she was certainly dim. Andrew was not as dim as she was, though he was not as bright as his two sisters or either of his parents: I suppose this may have been one of the causes of his curious social revolt. Usually I let her take the lead which, inferior or not, she was always quite ready to do, but upon this occasion it was clear to me that I must take the offensive.

"Having some friends round, are you?" I said briskly. "You don't often shop in town, do you?"

"Not very often," she said. "But I was in for the day, having my hair done."

"Oh, really? I'd tell you how nice it looks, but I can't really see with that hat. Where do you have it done?"

"Romain's. Where do you go?"

"I don't," I said. "It takes such a long time. Anyway, I believe in letting nature take its course. I don't like perms. Well, it seems a long time since I saw you; how's Andrew these days? Still as busy as ever?"

"Oh yes."

"Still playing bridge?"

"Yes," she smiled coldly, but meaning to be ingratiating, not cold, and then said bravely, "You must come over again one day. You couldn't make it last time I rang, I remember. It was Christmas, wasn't it, when I rang?"

"Oh," I said, "I'm afraid I'm frightfully busy these days. I doubt if I'll have time before the autumn." It was then February.

She looked away, nervously, with some embarrassment. I, too, was embarrassed but I wasn't going to show it.

"I'd better get on with my shopping," she said. "These dinner parties are a frightful bore."

"They must be," I said. "I don't know why you have them. Well, it has been nice seeing you, Clare. Do give my love to Andrew, won't you? Tell him you saw me, won't you?"

As I said this, I looked at her hard, wondering whether she would tell him what she had seen: she flushed slightly and did not meet my eyes, but I guessed that she would not tell him and found later that my guess was right. It was not to protect me that she restrained herself, I am sure, but rather to avoid having to take any possible action on my account. She did not like our family, with reason, and the less she saw of us the better she was pleased. As I left her, she was bending over the counter, pointing at a dressed pheasant with a plum-gloved hand: I walked away, thinking of her dinner parties and her endless visits to the dry cleaners and her sessions under the hairdryer. I have never been able to cure myself of the view that people who spend time at the hairdresser's spend it there because they have nothing better to do, and no other way of getting rid of their money: pitiable enough, oh yes, but I was sick of pity, and I preferred the indulgence of dislike. An idle parasite, that's what she is, I said to myself bitterly, as I walked home with my three-pound bag of flour, and I thought of my mother, her mouth full of hairpins, screwing her long thick hair up into its everlasting knot, while at the same time going through her day's reports from the probation center. My mother and Beatrice and I were all prettier than this girl, as well as being brighter: but Oh God, I thought, as I reached the lift and pushed the button, whose fault is that, whose fault, whose virtue, and my dislike ebbed away in a dry withdrawing scraping tide of equity, leaving me as ever on the hard damp shore of sociological pity.

Riches are a dreadful blight, and poor Clare hadn't even got riches: all she had was gentility and inherited voice. I say "poor Clare" so often because she is an unhappy woman, but I am an unhappy woman myself, so she could well say, "poor Rosamund." Sometimes I wonder whether it is not my parents who are to blame, totally to blame, for my inability to see anything in human terms of like and dislike, love and hate: but only in terms of justice, guilt and innocence. Life is not fair: this is the lesson that I took in with my Kellogg's cornflakes at our family home in Putney. It is unfair on every score and every count and in every particular, and those who, like my parents, attempt to level it out are doomed to failure. Though when I would say this to them, fierce, argumentative, tragic, over the cornflakes, driven almost to tears at times by their hopeless innocence and aspirations, they would smile peaceably and say, Yes, dear, nothing can be done about inequality of brains and beauty, but that's no reason why we shouldn't try to do something about economics, is it?

Of course, by any reasonable standards, we were rich enough ourselves: there was no real money in the family, nothing like what I later met at Cambridge, and with Roger, or even with self-made Joe, but nevertheless we were quite all right. My parents grumbled incessantly, but they did not go without. It took me a very long time to piece together an economic view of my own, owing partly to the anomalies of my upbringing, which had made me believe in the poor without being of them: I went to a very good grammar school, where again I was in the curious position of being the only child who would admit to Labour-voting parents, although my parents were among the poshest and most well-known of all. I knew that this was upside-down and I was confused by it. I remember very clearly the way in which I put together my picture of the rest of the world, the way I accumulated evidence about the way that others lived. There was one incident in particular which I recognized at the time to be a milestone of some kind: I must have been eight or nine and Beatrice a couple of years older. We had gone to a local park, accompanied by a girl whom I hesitate to describe as maid or nanny: she was eighteen or so, and peculiarly incompetent, as were all our domestic staff, and when she took us out she would always take us to the same park as she was having an affair with one of the gardeners. We knew all about this because she told us. She told us some horrific things.

It suited us very well because it left us free to follow our own amusements: our craze at that time was fishing. Armed with a net and a jam jar, we could catch minnows and tadpoles: it was very exciting.

On this spring afternoon, Beatrice and I left Marleen giggling in the shrubbery and made our way to a private little muddy bit of pond that we usually had to ourselves. This time, however, there were some boys there. We looked at them suspiciously, as we were used to being taunted by rough boys, but they seemed busy enough, so we got on with our fishing. We were unusually successful in our work; we caught a large dashing pink and blue stickleback. We greeted our catch with screams of delight, which attracted the attention of the two boys, who came over and inspected the fish as it thrashed frantically round its jar. They admired it and asked us how we got it and advised us to cover the jar. "They jump right out sometimes," one of them said. "They can jump ever so high. Like salmon, they jump." Then, all four of us together, we tried to find another one, while they told us about a female stickleback that they had kept for months in an old bucket. "We let her out in the winter," they said. "We brought her back here and let her out. We thought it might freeze up in our yard."

Beatrice and I were impressed by this evidence of sensibility, unusual in boys: they were nice boys and might well have been middle-class children like ourselves, being clad as we were in rather muddy trousers, jerseys and sandals. We were no experts in accents in those days. We all got on together very well, though we caught no more sticklebacks but only a couple of tiddlers. After an hour or so we were visited by a group of ducks and Beatrice remembered that we had been given some crusts for them: she got out our paper bag and started to hurl lumps into the water but the ducks, fat and overfed, were not interested. Not so, however, the two boys: after two pieces had been inspected and refused by the ducks, the smaller of the two, who looked endearingly like an illustration in Richmal Crompton said, "I say, can I have a bit?" Beatrice handed him the bag and he and his brother ate the lot. We were unsurprised, having eaten more eccentric things at school in our time; we continued to fish. Five minutes later, however, we heard Marleen calling: she could not see us as we were crouching on a bit of muddy bank, concealed from view by a few sooty, filthy laurels. We groaned and made a few childish jokes about how she'd been getting on with Dick. "That's not your Mum, is it?" asked the larger boy, as Marleen continued to yell our names, though without urgency.

"No, no," I said, horrified by the idea that Marleen could be anybody's mother. "No, she's just the maid." People were called maids in those days, even in our household: I did not think twice about using the word then, though I think twice about putting it in writing now. The two boys looked startled by this remark and one of them said, "Blimey then, are you rich?" Just that, precisely that. Beatrice and I suddenly saw the situation for what it was and looked at each other in alarm, ready to run and duck from any threatening stones; but there were no stones. Beatrice and I started hotly to deny our richness; we did not think ourselves rich, being, as we were, so much poorer than so many other people we knew, businessmen's daughters and such like, but we knew where we stood with these boys, and we were full of fright. But the boys did not mind; they liked us, they had enjoyed the afternoon, they were interested, impressed. They were, as Shaw might have said, the deserving and not the undeserving poor: nice boys, well-brought-up boys. But Beatrice and I knew that for our part, we were not deserving: we had not deserved their kind interest, but their contempt. We told them about Marleen and her boy friend, in hurried relief, and then we left them. "We might see you again," the boys said, but we knew that we would not. An hour like that in a lifetime is quite as much as one can expect. I have often thought of how they ate those crusts, not famished, not starving, but with eagerness nevertheless. And I had not known; in the future I felt that it would be my duty to know.

Years later, in fact quite recently, I went to stay with Beatrice and her family for a couple of nights: she had only two children then, the eldest four and the younger three. I liked them, though I did not understand them, and I would take them out for walks, and to pick black-berries: it was October. The research establishment where Hallam worked was on top of a hill, and I remember then the whole countryside was parched, bleached and silvery: the fields were full of pale stubble and there was no colour anywhere. They lived on a little mushroom housing estate, rather like an army camp; Beatrice's house was pleasant to live in, though quite uninteresting from without. They had one of the nicer ones. After lunch on the Sunday, Hallam, Beatrice and I were sitting in the drawing room in a tired stupor, amidst the creased and confused pages of several Sunday papers, when we heard a sudden sound of shouting from the garden outside where the children were playing. Beatrice dragged herself to her feet and went and looked through the window: "Oh Lord," she said, "not again," and with an expression of resigned anger went out and through the back door. By this time I too had got up to watch through the window: I saw Beatrice arrive at the front gate, detach from it her own two children, and say crossly to a small child hanging onto the other side of it, "Now then, off you go, be off." As she spoke, her voice lost its customary gentility and took on a certain harshness, the tone in which one might speak to a cat or dog. Then she started to pull her own two children away; they went willingly enough, though with backward glances of min-gled triumph and shame. I heard them all three come into the kitchen and then the sounds of removing of wellingtons, wiping of hands and so on; meanwhile I continued to watch through the window the small child whose arrival had caused such action and alarm.

She was a perfectly ordinary-looking little girl, clad in a pair of brown corduroy trousers, an old, rather overwashed jersey, and a pair of plastic shoes, the kind that are bad for the feet. She had a square, unexpressive face, and she watched the departure of Nicholas and Alexandra with unperturbed solidity, batting not an eyelid at Beatrice's dismissive tone. She did not go away, however, but continued to hang on the gate, staring into the garden, her face quite blank; until, quite suddenly, she burst into violent screaming tears, her face contorting and turning red as her jersey, her whole body shaking with emotion. I watched this display with some detachment, until her grief found words: then she started to bellow, in a frighteningly loud voice, "I haven't got nobody to play with, I haven't got nobody to play with." She yelled this several times until Beatrice re-emerged from the kitchen and shouted, once more, "Off you go": then she stopped shouting as suddenly as she had started, climbed down off the gate, and ran off.

A few minutes later, when Beatrice had persuaded her two to go upstairs and play in the playroom, she rejoined us in the drawing room; she came in, looking rather worn, and sank down on to the settee. Consumed with curiosity, I asked:

"What on earth was all that about?" and she proceeded to explain that the small child was the daughter of one of the menials connected with the establishment, and that she was forever pestering Nicholas and Alexandra to play with her, which they were not allowed to do.

"Why ever not?" I asked, and there was doubtless a note of accusation in my voice, for Beatrice replied crossly:

"Oh, it's all very well, but it really is quite impossible. I let them play at first but it was just out of the question, you've no idea of the kinds of things they got up to."

"No, you're too right, I haven't," I said, even more curious. "Do tell me."

"Well," she said, "I suppose I don't really mind accents and things, at least in theory, though that child is quite incomprehensible, she speaks in such an extraordinary fashion, but it's all the other things really that I just can't stand."

"Such as what?" I said.

"Oh, things like playing in the outside lavatory. I could never get them out of it. I was having to chase them out all the time. What they used to get up to in there God alone knows, I don't like to think. And then she taught them such frightful words; they had one wonderful game which consisted of swinging on the garden gate and yelling Silly Bugger at everyone that went by."

I laughed, and so did Beatrice, but she then went on, "It's all very well, but people don't like it, and then they teach it to other children, and so on, and in the end our kids won't have anyone left to play with but her, because the other parents won't put up with it even if I do, and I can hardly have mine ostracized for the sake of that, can I? Anyway, I don't mind 'silly bugger' so much, I've heard those particular words used by some quite respectable people in my time, it's all the other silly words I can't stand."

"What words?" I said, but Beatrice waved her hands dismissively and would not tell. I pressed her a little but all she would say was:

"Oh, they're not *bad* words, not the real shockers that all one's classy friends use, the ones the Lord Chamberlain doesn't like, just silly horrid childish vulgar words, and they think they're so funny and they shout them out and then go into fits of giggles."

It did sound peculiarly irritating, even to one as unconcerned as myself, but I felt myself constrained to say:

"They'd grow out of it, wouldn't they?"

"I suppose so," said Beatrice, "but in the meantime I've got to live."

"Even so," I said, "I think it ought to be against your principles. I'm sure upper-class children are just as silly and vulgar and horrid, aren't they?"

"Well, actually, they are, but they're silly in a way I can deal with, and I know how to stop them. I can't do anything with that child but shout at her."

"Why is she so keen to play with yours?"

"I don't know, really, I suppose it must be because all the bigger children go to the village school, and she's just too young, so there's no one left for her to play with round here. It's quite a different thing in the school holidays, then all the little toughs line up outside our gate, with her among them, and chuck stones at my kids. So what can I do? I don't see what I can do."

"What's her name?" I asked, and she said, with deep feeling:

"Sandra. Her name's Sandra. I really don't see what else I could do."

I didn't see what she could have done, either, though I think I might have tried to stick it out myself: and I often thought of Sandra, square and yelling, and thought what a pity it was that resentments should breed so near the cradle, that people should so have had it from birth.

My baby was due in early March: I amused myself by trying to finish my thesis before my baby. It was in fact somewhat of a hopeless task, as I was not even expected to finish it before the following Christmas, but I have always been a quick worker and now I had very little else to distract me. As the winter wore on, and spring set in, I felt less and less like going out, even as far as to the British

Museum, and I organized myself so that I could do a good deal of work at home. It was less entertaining than working in the library, but I could at least get on with it. It was all shaping up quite nicely; my director of studies, a don in Cambridge, had approved my synopsis, rough draft, first chapter, and other indications of the final product, and had been most encouraging. I felt happy about it; I had got it all into shape in my head and knew more or less exactly what I was going to say and what ground I had to cover. Then, towards the end of January, I began to flag. Although I would not admit it, I felt at times too tired to read. I ate more and more iron pills but they did not seem to have much effect. In the end I decided that I had merely got stale through too much concentration on too few things, and that I ought to branch out a little. It was, however, impossible to find anything amusing to do; I did not enjoy walking any more, public transport was a continual trial, I could not sit comfortably through a full-length picture, and I could not eat anything interesting without suffering for it afterwards. I felt thoroughly annoyed; I could understand, in this condition, why women are, as they certainly are, such perpetual complaining bores. I was discussing my problem with Lydia one evening; she suggested all sorts of occupations, like knitting, or rug-making, or basketwork, or weaving, but I rejected all these pseudo-useful employments with contempt. Then she said, finally, why don't you do jigsaw puzzles: and they were what I took up.

One can, if one tries, buy extremely complicated jigsaw puzzles with a thousand interlocking pieces, and pictures by old masters, or of ships at sea, and heaven knows what: also puzzles in the shape of maps of Europe, square puzzles, circular puzzles, star-shaped puzzles, reversible puzzles, anything one can imagine in the way of puzzles. I became addicted and would spend hours over them; it was a soothing, time-consuming process, and when I went to bed I would dream not of George, nor of babies locked away from me where I couldn't feed them, nor even of childbirth, but of pieces of blue sky edged with bits of tree, or small blue irregular shapes composing the cloak of the Virgin Mary. Lydia had an irritating habit of coming in at the end of an evening, just when I had mastered the most difficult part of a puzzle, and putting in all the easy obvious middle pieces; I got very annoyed with her. As a therapy, it worked extremely well; I found I could write my book and do a puzzle for alternate hours without getting unduly bored by either.

I suppose the end of anyone's first pregnancy is frightening. I cannot quite remember how frightened I was, because it is one of the horrible tricks of nature to make one forget instantly after childbirth all that one had feared and suffered, presumably so that one will carry on gaily with the next. In the same way one will protect with the utmost care an unborn child which one does not want and would prefer to lose, and which indeed as in my case may even have taken some steps, however feeble and ill-informed, towards losing; in January, after a party, I slipped on the stairs going down from a friend's flat and would certainly have fallen had I been in anything like my normal state of balance: but as it was I clutched and hung on to the banisters like grim death and got away with a mere twisted ankle. And thus, unwillingly, I have forgotten how worried I must have been, because it now seems so long ago and to have so little importance. I was worried partly through ignorance, as I had deliberately found nothing out about the subject at all, and had steered clear of all natural childbirth classes, film strips of deliveries, and helpful diagrams, convinced that I had only to go near a natural childbirth class in order to call down upon myself the most phenomenally unnatural birth of all time. There was no point in tempting providence, I thought; one might as well expect the worst as one would probably get it anyway.

I remember, however, the night before it was born with some clarity. It was not due for another week so I was not particularly worried; I boiled myself a couple of eggs, then went to eat them in the sitting room at about half past eight, and got out my typewriter at the same time in order to read over the last page of thesis that I had left inside it. When I opened the typewriter, however, it was not a page of discussion on Drayton's use of irony that met my eyes, but a page of something quite different, and not written by me at all. I knocked the top off my egg and started to read it, assuming, and rightly, that it was something of Lydia's; she had been complaining for weeks that her machine was going wrong. It was indeed something of Lydia's; it was a page from her next novel, which she had started shortly after moving in with me and which she had been working on, intermittently, ever since. I read the page with fascinated alarm; it was in the first person, and it was about a girl having an illegitimate baby. When I had finished the page, I abandoned my eggs and went into Lydia's bedroom to look for more. I found it, in a heap of loose leaves by her bed, and carried it back with me and sat down on the settee and started to read it.

I read the whole lot straight off, or what there was of it; it was not finished. It was nothing more nor less than my life story, with a few minor alterations here and there, and a few interesting false assumptions amongst the alterations. Clearly Lydia, for instance, had always assumed that Joe was the father of the child; there was an interesting though cleverly concealed portrait of Joe, and an absorbing scene in which the character that was me quarrelled violently with him and left him forever. Her motives for this I thought a little farfetched; she had apparently discovered that he was still sleeping with his mislaid wife, whom she had had the privilege of meeting, which was more than I had. This discovery had enraged her to such an extent that she had broken with him and refused any financial assistance from him. She had been planning to have the child only on the assumption that she and the Joe-character would live together and bring it up between them. Far-fetched as the theory seemed with regard to me, who did not know what the word jealousy meant, and indeed suffered from its opposite, if it has one, it certainly explained a possible line of conduct: it amused me to think of Lydia sitting there racking her brains trying to work out why I was having the child, and why I hadn't got rid of it. She had been inefficient enough on that score herself, by her own account, but then one never suspects that others share one's own degree of incompetence in such matters.

At first, for the first few chapters, I flattered myself that I emerged rather well—independent, strong-willed, and very worldly and *au fait* with sexual problems. An attractive girl, I thought. But then, as the chapters wore on, I began to have my doubts. Like myself, the character was engaged in academic research, an activity which Lydia appeared to regard with thorough contempt: she had invented for me a peculiarly meaningless and abstruse research subject, in fact none less than the ill-famed Henryson. I remembered I had told Lydia about my Indian in some detail and she had laughed with me about him. I could not, however, be too indignant as I have always been aware that the Elizabethans, except for Shakespeare, are somewhat of a luxury subject, unlike nineteenth-century novelists or prolific Augustan poets. However, I did object very strongly to the way, subtle enough technically, that she hinted that the Rosamund character's obsession with scholarly detail and discovery was nothing more nor less than an escape route, an attempt to evade the personal crises of her life and the realities of life in general. She drew a very persuasive picture of the academic ivory tower; whenever anything unpleasant happened to this character, as in the course of the extant ten chapters was too frequently the case, she would retire to bed or the British Museum with a pile of books, as others retire perhaps with a bottle of gin. There was also a long discussion on this very topic between the girl and a friend of hers, who presumably represented vitality, modernity, honesty and so on; I was not malicious enough to consider this a self-portrait of Lydia, for it clearly was not, as the girl friend in question was not like anyone I have ever met. She accused the me-character of having a jigsaw puzzle mind, a nasty crack in the circumstances, I thought; she herself was busy frittering her life away in vital pursuits like serving in a theater bar, working on a magazine, and having an affair with a television producer.

All in all, by the time I had finished this work I was both annoyed and upset. I did not think this view of scholarship at all justifiable; I could not produce my reasons for believing in its value, but in a way I was all the surer for that, for I knew it for a fact. Scholarship is a skill and I am good at it, and even if one rated it no higher than that it is still worth doing. Whether I used it as an escape or not was a different matter, and did not seem to me to be as relevant. It was work, and I did it, and reasons did not come into it; *il faut cultiver notre jardin,* as Voltaire so admirably said. Apart, however, from being annoyed by this attack on my livelihood, I was also very annoyed by the thought that Lydia had been living in my house for nothing and writing all this about me without saying a word. She had compared herself once to a spider, an image not wholly new, drawing material from its own entrails, but this seemed to me to be a somewhat more parasitic pursuit.

After rereading certain passages, I put the whole lot back by her bed, including the sheet that had been in my typewriter; I had no intention of saying anything to her but I thought it possible she might remember where she had left it and suffer from her own conclusions. Then I went back and sat down by the fire and switched on the radio, just in time to hear George talking about next Sunday's concert. I thought how odd it was that I had bumped into Clare at Selfridge's but had not even set eyes in the last eight months on George. I switched off again when he had finished announcing as my thoughts kept reverting to Lydia, with decreasing anger. After all, I thought, she had been making herself very useful recently, doing all the heavy shopping, even the odd few minutes' Hoovering, and had, moreover, acquired through a friend of hers a woman who had volunteered to come in and mind the baby two days a week when I was well enough to go out. In fact, lately I had even come to think myself slightly in her debt, despite the disadvantageous rent situation: and here, at least, in those pages of typescript had been proof that I was still the donor, she still the recipient. More than ever now I had the upper hand; she had got her money's worth but of me. Do not think I resented this: on the contrary, looking at our relationship in this light, I felt much happier, for I saw that we had maintained a basis of mutual profit. Having arrived at this conclusion, I thought I would go to bed, and when I got up I found I was suffering from distinct pains in the back.

Once I noticed that I was feeling them, I realized that I had been feeling them for quite a long time without paying them much attention. I instantly took them to be what, in fact, they were and was overcome with panic as it seemed such an inconvenient time to have to disturb hospital and ambulance men. It was a quarter past eleven, a time for all good citizens to be asleep. I was in a dilemma: the pains were not yet at all bad and I could clearly hang on at home for some time, but on the other hand the longer I waited the more inconvenient would grow the hour and the more irritable the nurses, midwives and ambulance people that I would have to encounter. I went to the bedroom and got out my little leaflet of instructions which told me to time the contractions and to ring the hospital when they became regular and more frequent than once every quarter of an hour. So I started to time them, and found to my alarm that they were perfectly regular and occurring once every three minutes. At half past eleven I rang the hospital, who told me to take an aspirin or two and ring the ambulance. So I did. Then I got out my suitcase, prepacked to order, put on my coat and waited. The men arrived within ten minutes, at exactly the same moment as Lydia who was returning home rather gay after a party. When she discovered my state and destination, she flung her arms around me, kissed me several times, and accompanied me downstairs in the lift, telling me en route about the party and how she had met Joe Hurt there, and how they had talked about me, and he had yet another book finished, and how fond of me he was, and how concerned, and how perhaps she quite liked him after all, and she would let him know instantly about the baby, whatever it turned out to be: the ambulance men and I listened to her story in solid quiet, but I was glad to have her there to stop my having to say things like It's a fine night, isn't it, or Sorry to disturb you at this hour, to these two silent men. Lydia looked rather weird, as her hair was coming down and she had lipstick all over one cheek: also she was wearing a strange long green lace dress and over it her usual grey mackintosh. She had no other coat. Her preoccupation with the subject of Joe I found illuminating, and I was glad to be able to put together, on new evidence, an attitude of hers that I had never understood.

I was glad too to be going from so good an address. I felt that by it alone I had bought a little deference and, sure enough, at the bottom of the stairs one of the men turned to Lydia and said, "Would you like to come along, Miss, to see your friend in?" He was rather taken by her, I could see, and her eyes too lit up at the prospect of so strange an excursion, but I said firmly that I would be better off on my own, it was only just down the road, I couldn't dream of disturbing her, what she needed was a good sleep. I did not fancy the idea of the details of my labour becoming available to her professional curiosity: she could have a baby herself, I thought, if she really wanted to know what it was like. She stood on the pavement and waved good-bye, shouting good luck after me as the ambulance drew away; she was an odd and charming sight in her strangely tiered garments.

On the way to the hospital I thought how unnerving it is, suddenly to see oneself for a moment as others see one, like a glimpse of unexpected profile in an unfamiliar combination of mirrors. I think I know myself better than anyone can know me, and I think this even in cold blood, for too much knowing is my vice; and yet one cannot account for the angles of others. Once at a party I met a boy whom I had known at school, and not seen since; we both had known that the other would be present and I had recognized him at once, but when we met and talked he confessed that when looking out for me he had taken another girl to be me. I asked him which, and he had pointed through the crowd at a tall, skinny girl with too-neat hair and a shut, frightened face: I was amazed and oddly hurt by his near-mistake, for she was so utterly unlike me, so devoid of any of my qualities or defects. And yet she was the same height, the same colouring, and, looking back, I could see that there was enough in me at sixteen that could have developed that way and that in six years sixteen-year-old Rosamund Stacey might well have been her and not me.

When we arrived at the hospital, I thought with some relief that this would be my last visit, and that at the least the clinic was over with all its eroding grind. I climbed out of the ambulance and started off down the corridor, but one of the men stopped me and said that I had to go in a wheelchair. What do you mean, I said, I can walk.

"You're not allowed to walk," he said.

"Why ever not?" I asked, not because I objected to going in a wheelchair, but because I couldn't see why not. "I walked at the other end," I said.

"Ah yes," said the man, "but at this end you're not allowed to. Come along now, you're our responsibility now, we can't allow you to walk, I'm afraid."

So I sat down, succumbing to his threat that he would lose his job if I didn't, and they wheeled me off down countless corridors, up in a lift, down a floor in another one, and into a large room where I was told to get up and go and sign a list. Here, it seemed, I was allowed to walk. I had been expecting to see a few familiar faces, such as the thin little Yorkshire nurse, the fat Irish one, or even the smart red-haired midwife; I had, luckily in the event, no grandiose expectations of seeing any doctors or gynecologists. But there was not a face I recognized in sight: a whole new army of people appeared to have taken over, who presumably came out only at night. I was a little disappointed; the other faces had become almost endeared by familiarity. I signed my name on the relevant register; the nurse in charge of it looked up and said, "Well, you're the only one in tonight, we *were* having a quiet night," and I smiled feebly, unsure whether she was expressing pleasure or annoyance at having something to do.

Then they took me off to another room and took away all my clothes and put me in a hospital nightgown and asked me how often my contractions were. When I told them, they said Nonsense, but when they investigated they naturally enough found me to be right. Then they did various other unpleasant and compulsory things, found me my book when I asked for it, and left me to it, telling me to ring if I wanted anything. I lay there on this hard high bed for half an hour, trying to read, and then I rang the bell and asked if they couldn't do something about it. Not yet, they said, and off they went. I lay there for another ten minutes and then a quite different nurse came in and said I had to move, somebody else had to have my bed. I lay there and looked at her and said how. Don't you feel like walking, she said, and I said Oh, all right, as she seemed to expect me to, and I heaved myself down off this mountainously high iron bedstead and followed her down a corridor and into another room, where she helped me on to an equally high identical bed. Then I asked once more, politely, if they couldn't do something about it, and she said Oh yes, of course, wasn't it time I had some pethidine, and she would go and find someone to give me an injection.

A quarter of an hour later about five nurses arrived with the pethidine, which they administered; then they all sat in a row in the corridor outside and started to talk about their boy friends. I listened to their conversations, trying to distract myself from sensations that did not seem quite reasonable or endurable, and after a while the drug began to work: the pain did not diminish but my resistance to it disappeared, and every two minutes regularly it flowed through me as thought I were some other person, and as though I myself, what was left of me, was watching this swell and ebb from many miles away. It was no longer personal and therefore bearable; I just lay there and let it happen, and the voices of the five girls came to me very clearly and purely, the syntax and connections of their dialogue illuminated by a strange pale warm light. One of them started off by telling the others about some character called Frank, against whom the others had apparently been warning her for some time, for when she described the way in which he had squeezed her knee in the cinema, the others began to exclaim with predestined admiring indignation.

"Honestly, I *told* you what he was like," one of them

said, "I *told* you what he'd be up to, didn't I? You should have heard what Elaine said about him after the Christmas Ball."

"Elaine asks for it," said another voice, and they all giggled, and somebody else said, "Well, you don't exactly go out of your way to avoid it yourself, do you? I mean to say, what *about* that dress you had on the other day? If that wasn't a topless dress, I'd like to know what is."

"Do you know *what*," said the owner of the dress, "happened to me last time I was wearing it? I had to dash home, it was a Thursday and I hadn't got a late leave, and I *just* got to the corner of Charles Street at eleven-thirty, and I had to run like anything, and anyway I just got to the door as Bessie was locking up and I got in all right, but who do you think I met on the other side but Mrs. Sammy Spillikins, all in her dressing gown and slippers, and she gave me such a look and said in that voice of hers, you know what she sounds like, Well, well, well, Miss Ellis, she said, you do cut things rather fine, don't you? Are you in the habit of leaving things to the last moment like this? Mean old cow, I'd like to know what it's got to do with her. And she said she wanted a word, and she followed me all the way up to my room, just on the pretext of asking me some question about what Dr. Cohen asked Gillian to do about the new radiator in the waiting room, and she stayed so long I had to take my coat off, and she kept looking and looking at me, and when she left do you know what she said? She said, In my day, with a dress like that, we used to wear modesty vests."

Once more they all giggled merrily, and then someone volunteered the information that however old Sammy Spillikins looked, she was really only forty-two, which she had on the best of authority, and somebody else described, though as a matter of fact inaccurately, what a modesty vest was, when one of the gathering claimed not to know.

"How *disgusting*," the ignorant one said vehemently when enlightened.

They then told some more anecdotes about their evidently circumscribed love lives before moving on to discuss their trade. They began mildly enough by inquiring how many had been born the night before, and what had happened to the little premature one that was failing earlier in the evening, but after a while the tone really became too extreme for my possible comfort; they described cases of women who had lain in labour for unbelievable lengths of time, of one who had screamed solidly for three hours, of a black woman who had scratched a nurse's face when she tried to give her an enema, of a white woman who had sworn at one of the black nurses and told her to get out, she wasn't having her filthy hands on her nice clean new baby. One of them said, *en passant,* "I'll be really glad to get out of this ward. I don't really mind the babies, but the mothers are enough to give anyone the creeps." Then one of them started to recount in vivid detail the story of a woman whose labour she had attended a month earlier, who had died because they discovered at the last moment that this that and the other hadn't been properly dealt with; "it was awful," this girl said, "the way they kept on telling her it was all fine, and I could see them getting bluer and bluer, you know how they look when anything really bad starts up." At this I could take it no longer, and I heard my voice yell, from a long way away, "Oh, for God's sake, pack it in, can't you?"

I don't think they caught what I said despite my unnatural loudness of tone, but two of them came bustling in and said, "What was that, did you call, how are you getting on?"

"I think this drug thing must be wearing off," I said mildly, "because it seems to be getting worse and worse, can you give me something else please, quick?"

"Oh no!" they said, "not yet, you've a long time to go yet, we have to leave something to give you later on."

"Oh," I said feebly, "what a pity."

"Never mind," they said, "you're coming along nicely," and they turned and went back to their row of seats outside and had just resumed their conversation, though in more muffled tones, when I heard myself start to moan rather violently, and they all came rushing back and within five minutes my child was born.

Right up to the very last minute, through sensations which though unbelievably violent were now no longer painful but indeed almost a promise of pleasure, I could hear them arguing among themselves, all of them; one had been dispatched for the midwife, one was looking for the gas and air, one was asking the others why they hadn't believed what I said, and another, while delivering the baby, had taken upon herself the task of calmer and soother of my nerves.

"That's all right," she kept saying, "that's fine, you're coming along fine. Oh, do try not to push."

There was more panic in her smooth tones than in me; I felt all right now, I felt fine. The child was born in a great rush and hurry, quite uncontrolled and undelivered; they told me afterwards that they only just caught her, and I felt her fall from me and instantly sat up and opened my eyes, and they said, "It's a girl, it's a lovely little girl."

They told me to lie down again, and I lay down, asking if the baby was all right, expecting suddenly I don't know what, missing arms and fingers, and they said she was all right; so I lay there, happy that it was over, not expecting they would let me see her, and then I heard her cry, a strange loud sobbing cry. The midwife had by now arrived, all smiles and starch, and actually apologized for not having been there. "It was quite a case," she said, "of too many cooks spoil the broth, you know, but you certainly managed to do all right without me, didn't you?" All the nurses too were suddenly humanized; they clustered round, helping to wash me and straighten me out, and telling me how unbelievably quick I'd been, and how I should have made more fuss, and that it was only half past two, and what was I going to call the baby. This last question was hastily silenced by the midwife, who presumably assumed the child would not be mine for long, but I did not care. I felt remarkably well, a usual reaction I believe on such occasions, and I could have got up and walked away. After ten minutes or so, when I had been returned to my own nightdress, a garment covered in Mexican embroidery which Beatrice had sent specially for the occasion, and which drew screams of admiration from the girls, the midwife asked me if I would like to see the child. "Please," I said gratefully, and she went away and came back with my daughter wrapped up in a small grey blood-stained blanket, and with a ticket saying Stacey round her ankle. She put her in my arms and I sat there looking at her, and her great wide blue eyes looked at me with seeming recognition, and what I felt it is pointless to try to describe. Love, I suppose one might call it, and the first of my life.

I had expected so little, really. I never expect much. I had been told of the ugliness of newborn children, of their red and wrinkled faces, their waxy covering, their emaciated limbs, their hairy cheeks, their piercing cries. All I can say is that mine was beautiful and in my defense I must add that others said she was beautiful too. She was not red nor even wrinkled, but palely soft, each feature delicately reposed in its right place, and she was not bald but adorned with a thick, startling crop of black hair. One of the nurses fetched a brush and flattened it down and it covered her forehead, lying in a dense fringe that reached to her eyes. And her eyes, that seemed to see me and that looked into mine with deep gravity and charm, were a profound blue, the whites white with the gleam of alarming health. When they asked if they could have her back and put her back in her cradle for the night, I handed her over without reluctance, for the delight of holding her was too much for me. I felt as well as they that such pleasure should be regulated and rationed.

When they had removed her, they wheeled me off to a ward and put me to bed and gave me some sleeping pills and assured me I would fall asleep at once and be out till the morning. But I didn't, I lay awake for two hours, unable to get over my happiness. I was not much used to feeling happiness: satisfaction, perhaps, or triumph, and at times excitement and exhilaration. But happiness was something I had not gone in for for a long time, and it was very nice, too nice to waste in sleep. I dozed off at about half past four but was awakened at half past five with cups of tea and the sight of all the other mothers giving their babies breakfast.

I tried to explain the other day to somebody, no less than Joe Hurt himself in fact, about how happy I had felt, but he was very contemptuous of my descriptions. "What you're talking about," he said, "is one of the most boring commonplaces of the female experience. All women feel exactly that, it's nothing to be proud of, it isn't even worth thinking about."

I denied hotly that all women felt it, as I knew hardly a one who had been as enraptured as I, and then I contradicted my own argument by saying that anyway, if all other women did feel it, then that was precisely what made it so remarkable in my case, as I could not recall a single other instance in my life when I had felt what all other women feel.

But it was no good arguing, Joe was just not interested; just as I was very little interested though occasionally amazed by his lengthy descriptions of the sexual ecstasies of his heroes. It is sad to be boring, but perhaps when I think how often I am bored, not quite as sad as it might be.

My stay in hospital was really quite entertaining. Fortified by the superior beauty and intelligence of my child (the latter manifested in such talents as learning to suck at the first attempt, and not after hours of humiliating struggle), I was able to withstand various irritations, such as having a label at the end of my bed with the initial U, which stood, I was told, for Unmarried, and a perpetual succession of medical students who kept taking my temperature and measuring various parts of me with cold wooden rulers and making feeble jokes. I was highly grateful to Lydia, who certainly did her best for me in broadcasting the news, for on the very first morning I received dozens of bouquets and telegrams, from everyone I had ever known, or rather from everyone that Lydia had ever known that I had known. It was a good time of year for flowers, and daffodils, tulips, roses, azaleas and Lord knows what appeared in vast profusion: I began to grow quite embarrassed, finally, thinking that such excess might annoy the nurse who kept bringing them in to me, or the other less gifted mothers.

In the visiting hour that evening, Lydia turned up, with Joe Hurt himself accompanying her; she was evidently proud of her skill in having got him there, and glowed with varying kinds of satisfaction as she sat on the end of my bed and thumbed her way through my Lydia-instigated pile of congratulations. They made a bizarre and impressive couple, splendidly out of key with the nature of the occasion; she in a black skirt and jersey, black stockings and patent shoes, and the everlasting uncleaned raincoat, he in a peculiar collarless suit and with a more than usually volcanic irregularity in his features. He had recently started appearing on an egghead television program, talking about culture, and some of the mothers recognized him, to his great gratification and, I must admit, to mine, for I felt my stock would rise through the association. They brought me a whole pile of books to read, and half a bottle of whisky wrapped up in some clean underwear; I was doubtful about accepting it, thinking the baby might not like it, but they told me not to be so foolish, alcohol was good for every system, any doctor would tell me.

I was very pleased to see Joe again; naturally we had met fairly frequently over the past few months, though always by chance, and with nothing like our former regularity. He was a great morale-raiser; he was interested in the set-up in the ward and asked me about the nurses and the other mothers and what did we talk about, and laughed gaily over the Unmarried notice on the end of my bed, as though it were the funniest thing he had ever seen. He kept lighting cigarettes, absent-mindedly, and a pretty Kensington blonde nurse, kept specially for visiting-hours display, would rush over each time and tell him it wasn't allowed, he would have to go out if he wanted to smoke. He showed no interest at all in the baby, who was lying by the side of my bed in a little cradle on wheels: Lydia's theory about his paternity must have suffered some shaking from this, as surely any father would volunteer his newborn infant at least a glance. After ten minutes or so, however, when I had told them as many details about my confinement as they could bear to hear, they began to discuss what name I should give the child. I had spared the subject little thought myself, as I do not like to anticipate, to count or name my chickens before they are hatched, and now I had seen her no name seemed good enough. They suggested names endlessly, ranging from the dull to the fantastic; Joe came down finally in favour of January, while Lydia seemed to fancy Charlotte, which I thought pretty but corny. After a long debate, they asked me what name I liked, and I said that I rather fancied Sandra myself. They roared with laughter once more, and all the other quietly muttering mothers and fathers became silent and stared, glad of a distraction, finding us as good as the telly.

In the end I said I would call her Octavia. I said it as a joke, having tried hard to think of some famous woman to call her after, and finding none but Beatrice Webb whom my parents had already used; the name Octavia Hill came into my mind, and I said out loud, I'll call her Octavia. Both of them seemed to approve, though they said she wasn't my eighth at all, and ought rather to be called Prima, though that wasn't so pretty; one might as well call her Ultima, poor child, I said, and have done with it.

"I don't know," said Joe, "if I were you, I'd have a few more. It seems to agree with you, you look astoundingly well."

"I feel well," I said, "but it wouldn't be worth doing it all over again just to feel well."

"Just one more," said Joe. "You're allowed two, you know."

"What do you mean, allowed two? By whom? Allowed by whom?"

"Oh, by authority. The BBC lets you have two before they sack you. So does the Civil Service. It's the orthodox number, two."

"Illegitimate ones, you mean?"

"Naturally. You can have as many as you like of the other ones, until they interfere with your efficiency."

"Why ever two?" I said. "It doesn't seem very reasonable, does it? Surely if they allow you more than one, they ought to allow you an unlimited number? I mean to say, I can understand them allowing one and no more, on the grounds that one might be an innocent mistake, but once you've allowed two, why not five or ten or eighteen? Anyway, is that true? I'm sure it's not true, it's just some rubbish some girl told you."

"A woman died," Lydia said, "last week, in *The Times,* of her twenty-fifth baby, in France."

"Sh," I said, glancing round at my fellow inmates. "You

don't know how many of these are on their twenty-fourth, do you?"

"When are your parents coming back?" said Joe. "Have you told them they've got a grandchild living in their house?"

"They're not due back till next Christmas, not for good," I said.

"It couldn't have been more convenient really, could it?" said Joe. "Anyone would think you'd worked it all out on purpose."

"Perhaps I did," I said. "Didn't you know, I'm one of those Bernard Shaw women who wants children but no husband? It suits me fine, like this."

"It seems to suit you," said Joe kindly. "I said you look extremely well. When you get up, you can get Lydia to baby-sit for us and I'll take you to the cinema."

But I could tell, from the way he was looking at Lydia, that it was she who would be sitting next to him in the back stalls for the next few months. And really, I thought, they went quite well together, balanced as they were delicately on social aspirations, rivalry, fashionability and dislike. They were well suited, I thought.

When they had gone, the woman from the next bed leaned over and said, "Isn't that young man an announcer on the television?"

I said that he wasn't an announcer but that he was on the television.

"I thought I'd seen him," she said. "I thought I'd seen him, that's all I wanted to know."

She was a vacant-faced, prematurely aging woman of thirty or so, in for her fourth child, and she spent most of her time knitting shapeless fancy-stitch cardigans for her mother, and trying to tell the woman on the other side about her other three children and what they ate and what they wouldn't touch. I wondered what she had thought of Joe's program; on the only edition I had seen he had been talking with some intensity about the dominance of drugs in modern literature to an anonymous, back-head-photographed drug addict. The other editions had been even less interesting than that, comprising such subjects as the future of abstract art and the use of improvisation in avant-garde Paris theater of today (topics on which Joe was quite unqualified to express any views at all).

The woman in the bed beyond the woman who had recognized Joe never listened to the stories of which child liked kippers and which preferred a little cheese on toast: she preferred to tell stories to the woman beyond her, about the best ways of dealing with a large family wash. The woman beyond her had to listen, as she was flanked by a brick wall, and I heard them at one moment engaged in the most exquisite deadlock: Woman B said to Woman C:

"Of course," she said, "there's nothing like soap flakes, that's what I've always said, these detergents are no good for anything, bring me out in spots, they do," to which Woman C retorted that soap flakes were no good in machines.

Woman B conceded the point, but then went on to say that there was nothing like washing by hand, really.

Woman C said that she went to the launderette.

Woman B said that launderettes were a great boon and no mistake, but then went on to expand the point that you never got results as good as when you washed at home by hand. Woman C, however, not perhaps paying as much attention as she might have done, misunderstood her, taking her to say that you never get results *as good when* you wash at home, not as *good as when;* she proceeded to agree with Woman B, or so she thought, producing a great panegyric on the virtues of machinery, the thoroughness of their washing, the frequency of their rinsing, the power of their spin drying, and to denigrate the effort, efficiency and end-product of hand-washing. Woman B, either not noticing her strange logic, or determined to ignore it, went on quite smoothly as soon as she could interrupt:

"Yes, of course, you're quite right, I do agree, and then the wear and tear of those machines is something terrible, you can put things in and they come out in ribbons. Now I can keep things for years. I had some pillowcases, embroidered ones, I'd washed them by hand in pure soap for ten years, and then my sister-in-law persuades me to put them in her machine, and when I get them out they're all frayed down the edges. It just shows you, doesn't it?"

"It certainly does," said Woman C. "I think it must be all that rubbing and scrubbing that does it, when you do it by hand you rub too hard, you know, no wonder things don't last, you can't expect them to last."

And so they might have gone on for hours, running side by side in smooth and never-touching incomprehension, had not Woman A, unable to bear her exclusion any longer, suddenly yelled to both of them, "Do yours eat spinach? You wouldn't believe the trouble I've had getting mine to eat spinach, and my husband, he loves it, but I can't go buying it just for him, can I?"

As it happened, I was the next to youngest in the ward; apart from one cheery teen-ager, all the other fourteen mothers were either nearly thirty or over it. The teen-age girl and I were the only ones in for our first, which seemed a statistical coincidence, but may not have been. She looked so like an unmarried mother that as soon as I was able to get up I made a pretext for hobbling past the end of her bed, but the label on it said M, not U. She really was cheery, the only person apart from me who ever seemed to smile, let alone laugh, with any real enthusiasm; she spent most of her time looking at herself in a small hand mirror, plucking her eyelashes, squeezing invisible blackheads, putting on lipstick, taking it off again, trying a different colour, painting her nails, and putting her hair in curlers so she would look nice for visiting time. Once I had noticed her, I looked out for her husband; he turned out to a sharp-faced little boy who looked and may well have been about sixteen. She and I exchanged glances of mutual curiosity, being the only people there with any pretensions to any physical charm; our beds were too far apart for us to converse, but we met once in the lavatories, where she had gone to smoke a quick cigarette. She offered me one, and I declined it, saying I didn't feel like smoking any more: she laughed, and said it was funny how one went off things, she'd gone right off drink, it had saved them a fortune. We went back into the ward together, and admired each other's babies, before retiring to our beds; she said mine was ever so lovely, though I could see her thinking her a funny, skimpy little thing, and I said hers was beautiful child, though to me he looked fat and bald, and bigger in some way than either of his narrow-faced parents. What we meant was, not that we liked each other's babies, but that we were glad that each other was there, as an ally against the older fatter women, so entirely and tediously submerged.

After the birth, the muscles of my belly snapped back into place without a mark, but some of the women looked as big as they had looked before. I am haunted even now by a memory of the way they walked, large and tied into shapeless dressing gowns, padding softly and stiffly, careful not to disturb the pain that still lay between the legs.

On my sixth day, the gynecologist came round, accompanied by his attendant students. They prodded me and questioned me and talked about me, and I felt oddly offended, for I was beginning to feel whole again and resented their interference, until the gynecologist said to his students, "Notice the resilience of the muscles here. This is the case that Hargreaves said would have an exceptionally small baby, but you see how wrong he was, it weighed a good six and a half pounds. He was taken in by the exceptional firmness of the muscle."

Then he turned to me and smiled and said, "Were you by any chance a professional dancer?"

I was taken so unawares by this direct question that I did not at first think that he was addressing me, and had to be startled out of my reverie by a repetition of the question.

"Good heavens no," I said, "nothing like that."

"You must have some athletic pursuits," he said.

"No, none at all," I said. "None at all."

"Then you must be just made that way," he said, and smiled and passed on. I glowed with satisfaction for half an hour afterwards, as though a medal for good conduct had been pinned to my lapel.

Lydia came to see me every evening, sometimes alone, sometimes accompanied by some friend to whom she had been able to sell the idea of a hospital visit as an evening's entertainment. My bedside was always more animated than those of the others, more like a party, and my gratitude to her for it was unlimited. On my last, ninth evening, however, she could not make it; she rang during the afternoon to leave a message, and I thought that I would not mind, but when the visiting time came and the shuffling, silent husbands arrived, I drew my flimsy curtain and turned my head into the pillow and wept. I kept telling myself as I wept that it was nothing, just reaction, that magic excuse for all affliction, and it probably was too, but none the less painful for that. I wanted to fish Octavia out of her small white cot and hold her, to comfort me, but it was not feeding time and I did not dare. I had been taught to get her out only at the correct intervals, and although I knew this method to be outdated, I did not like to break the rules. Also, the baby was asleep, and I did not see why I should wake her for my own comfort. So I put my head in the pillow, like a child anxious not to disturb its parents, and I cried.

Authority, the war, Truby King. I was reared to believe that the endurance of privation is a virtue, and the result is that I believe it to this day.

Actually, surprisingly enough, my stay in hospital was one of the more cheerful and sociable patches of my life. Except for that last evening, I did not for a moment feel lost or abandoned; nor, owing perhaps to my delight in the baby, did I feel that I was on the receiving end of pity and sympathy. I have always rather fancied the idea of holding a salon, of lying on a couch and dispensing charm and conversation to some favoured and intimate circle, though I have never made any approach towards it as a way of life, being a solitary, I suppose, a gregarious solitary, and those ten days, surrounded by flowers, and receiving much correspondence and many visitors every day, I felt as near to belonging to a circle as I have ever done. My ways and my acquaintances were defined, made more precious and more themselves, by contrast with those of the other women in the ward, and I could not but think that Beatrice had been ludicrously mistaken by her fears for the social position of my child. It seemed to me that anyone that I might be likely to know would be equally likely to take the situation without batting an eyelid. And here I must make clear that had I not been who I am, and born and reared as I was, I would probably never have dared: I only thought I could get away with it, to put it briefly, because those ambulance men collected me from a good address, and not from a bed-sitter in Tottenham or from a basement in ever-weeping Paddington. So, in a way, I was cashing in on the foibles of a society which I have always distrusted; by pretending to be above its strictures, I was merely turning its anomalies to my own use. I would not recommend my course of action to anyone with a shade less advantage in the world than myself. Though recommendation in such cases is luckily likely to have no effect whatsoever.

There is another point to be considered in my choice, and that is that I was equipped to earn my own living, forever, and in a trade that could be employed as well in a hospital bed as anywhere, or almost as well. Also, although I am diffident about the particulars of my qualifications, I suppose I must have a rock-like confidence in my own talent, for I simply did not believe that the handicap of one small illegitimate baby would make a scrap of difference to my career: I was in such a strong position by nature that were a situation to arise in which there were any choice to make between me and another, I would win, through the evident superiority of my mind. I felt that I was good enough to get away with it, and so far I must say that I have not been disproved. I finished my thesis in excellent time, it was published and praised in the right quarters, and thought much of by those who control my economic situation. And, moreover, I am a good teacher, having enthusiasm, yet expecting only what can be done. All this too is unfair, though perhaps less unfair than possessing an address in Marylebone, for I am industrious as well as equipped.

I left hospital in a taxi on the tenth day with Octavia in my arms and Lydia by my side. I was excited at the thought of getting home and having my baby to myself, but the cold of the outside air must have startled her, for she began to scream and screech violently in the taxi, and when we got home I did not quite know what to do. In hospital she had always been so quiet and sweet. I laid her down in her basket, but the mattress was a different shape from the hospital cot, and she looked strange and uncomfortable and screamed all the more fiercely. She looked odd, too, in her own Viyella nighties, after the regulation garments she had worn all her life until that afternoon. She went on and on crying, and I began to think that she would never adapt to real life. Lydia was getting almost as worried as I was, and after a while she said, as we both sat miserably and watched this small furious person, "Why don't you feed her? That would shut her up, wouldn't it?"

I looked at my watch; it was half past four.

"It's not time to feed her yet," I said. "In hospital, we had to feed them on the dot at five."

"Oh," said Lydia, "half an hour one way or the other can't make much difference."

"Don't you think so?" I said. "But then she'll wake half an hour early at the next feed, and the next, and the next, and then what will I do?"

"It wouldn't matter, would it?"

"I don't know. I somehow feel things would get all muddled and never get straight again. She was good and reasonable in hospital. And then she'll get confused, and how will she ever know when it's nighttime? How will she ever learn that it's night?"

"I should feed her," said Lydia. "It looks to me as though she's going to have a fit."

I didn't think she would have a fit, but I couldn't stand the sound of her crying, so I picked her out and fed her, and she became quiet at once, and fell asleep afterwards looking as though her mattress and nightdress were very comfortable after all. On the other hand, she did wake half an hour early at the next feed, and went on and on waking earlier, until we worked right back round the clock, for the truth was that she never went four hours but only three and a half. Looking back on it, it doesn't seem to matter at all, but it seemed very important at the time, I remember. It took her ages, moreover, to learn about night and day, and in the end I concluded that they had been giving her secret bottles in the night at the hospital.

However, on the whole, things worked out very well. I had a subsidized home help to begin with, and after a fortnight or so this woman whom Lydia had discovered, an amiable fat lady named Mrs. Jennings, came in two days a week while I dashed off to the library between feeds. Mrs. Jennings adored babies, and I found that all her chat about little darling tiny thingies, and where's her little tootsie wootsies, fell quite naturally and indeed gratefully upon my ears. I very shortly gave up feeding Octavia myself, as to my amazement I found the process quite infuriating and nervewracking: I stuck it for six weeks, hoping that as the more modern books said it would become a pleasure, or at least less of a drag, and the baby certainly seemed to enjoy it, but in the end I could stand it no longer and gave up. I didn't find the act itself disgusting, or anything like that, but the consequences were extremely messy; I grew frantic at the way my clothes got covered in milk, and in fact those six weeks have had a permanent effect on my life, for now I am as fussy as Clare about dirt, and am forever washing my clothes before they need it, sending things to the cleaners when I can't afford it, and paying secret nocturnal visits to the launderette. Also, despite evidence to the contrary, I could never believe that there was really anything there, that the baby was really getting anything at all to drink. What the eye doesn't see, I don't believe in, and the first time I gave her a bottle and watched the milk-level descending, ounce by careful ounce, I was overcome with relief, and I think I counted that as the first real meal of her life. Unnatural, I suppose, and I daresay we would have survived together in the desert, but just the same I was glad I had an alternative. Anyway, only posh middle-class mothers nurse these days, on principle, and I don't believe in principle. I believe in instinct, on principle.

Octavia was an extraordinarily beautiful child. Everyone said so, in shops and on buses and in the park, wherever we went. I took her to Regent's Park as often as I could face getting the pram up and down in the lift. It was a tolerable summer, and we both got quite brown. I was continually amazed by the way in which I could watch for hours nothing but the small movements of her hands, and the fleeting expressions of her face. She was a very happy child, and once she learned to smile, she never stopped; at first she would smile at anything, at parking meters and dogs and strangers, but as she grew older she began to favour me, and nothing gave me more delight than her evident preference. I suppose I had not really expected her to dislike and resent me from birth, though I was quite prepared for resentment to follow later on, but I certainly had not anticipated such wreathing, dazzling gaiety of affection from her whenever I happened to catch her eye. Gradually I began to realize that she liked me, that she had no option to liking me, and that unless I took great pains to alienate her she would go on liking me, for a couple of years at least. It was very pleasant to receive such uncritical love, because it left me free to bestow love; my kisses were met by small warm rubbery unrejecting cheeks and soft dovey mumblings of delight.

Indeed, it must have been in expectation of this love that I had insisted upon having her, or rather refrained from not having her: something in me had clearly known before I did that there would be compensations. I was not of course treated to that phrase which greets all reluctant married mothers, "I bet you wouldn't be without her now," so often repeated after the event, in the full confidence of nature, because I suppose people feared I might turn on them and say, Yes I certainly would, which would be mutually distressing for questioner and me. And in many ways I thought that I certainly would prefer to be without her, as one might reasonably prefer to lack beauty or intelligence or riches, or any other such sources of mixed blessing and pain. Things about life with a baby drove me into frenzies of weeping several times a week, and not only having milk on my clean jerseys. As so often in life, it was impossible to choose, even theoretically, between advantage and disadvantage, between profit and loss: I was up quite unmistakably against No Choice. So, the best one could do was to put a good face on it, and to avoid adding to the large and largely discussed number of sad warnings that abounded in the part of the world that I knew. I managed very well, and the general verdict was, Extraordinary Rosamund, she really seems happy, she must have really wanted one after all.

I had thought, dimly, that after the birth I would once more become interested in men, as such, but nothing like this seemed to happen. I did from time to time think that it would be comforting to have a little adult affection, but in some strange way I did not seem to like anyone enough any more. I felt curiously disenchanted, almost as I might have felt had I been truly betrayed and deceived and abandoned. The only person of whom I thought with any tenderness, apart from my small pliant daughter, was George. I still listened to his voice on the radio, comforted to know he was still so near, however pointlessly, and wondering what he was doing. Occasionally, when roused to a pitch of peculiar transport by Octavia's charm, I felt like ringing him up and telling him about her, but I never did; I fancied that I knew enough about human nature to know that no amount of charm could possibly balance the quite unjustified sense of obligation, financial, personal, and emotional, that such a revelation would instantly set to work. So I spared him and myself. Sometimes I thought I saw a likeness to him in Octavia, and more often I thought I caught a glimpse of George himself, but it was never him, it was always smooth young men selling things in antique shops or expensive tailors, who might have been him.

And so the summer wore away, and autumn set in, and the baby started to sit up, and I finished my thesis, and Lydia seemed to be on the verge of finishing her novel, though hampered by an affair with Joe, and I began to worry about what would happen at Christmas when my parents came home. This last problem worried me a good deal and I reached the point where I thought that I had only had the baby because I had had the flat. Autumn also brought other problems, such as the cold. I had never noticed the cold before, being healthy and energetic, but this year there was an unusually bitter October, with rain, fog, damp, and frost at nights. I did not mind for myself, but I did not know how to keep the baby warm; when I put gloves on her, she chewed them, and then had to ride around in her pram with icy wet hands. She dribbled, too, and her chest was always damp. She resisted for some time, but in the end she caught a cold. At first it did not seem to worry her, but then she started to wake coughing in the night, and when she breathed she wheezed terribly like an old sheep. I did not know what to do with her, as I hated going to the doctor; I had thought to have finished with my dreary, time-wasting association with the Health Service at her birth, though I had already discovered that there was an unending succession of injections, inspections, vaccinations and immunizations yet to be endured. But up to this point, everything had been routine, and not a matter of choice. Now, watching Octavia's nose run unbecomingly, and hearing her heavy spluttering, I knew I would have to decide to take her, and I found myself amazingly resistant to the idea. My reasons, I knew, were an inextricable mass of the selfish and the childishly diffident: I did not want to bother the busy doctor unnecessarily, having a great fear of bothering people, though perhaps more of a fear of being told that I am a nuisance, and I did not want to wait for two hours in a freezing cold waiting room with an active baby bouncing on my frail knee. It was not a simple choice between comfort and duty, and moreover it was not even my own health that was in question, but Octavia's. Had it been my own, I would never have gone.

About twenty-four hours after I had made up my mind

that I really ought to go, I consulted Lydia who at first was as perplexed by the problem as I was. She suggested that I should ring up the doctor and ask him to come and see me, instead of going to him; I had never even thought of doing this, which shows how little I had come to terms with the facts of my new life, and immediately thought how very nice it would be if only I dare.

"Of course you dare," said Lydia. "That's what doctors are there for. You can't take the child out in weather like this, in that condition."

"There's probably nothing wrong with her at all," I said miserably. "They never give babies anything for colds, anyway."

"I know what," said Lydia with a sudden illumination. "Why don't you take her temperature?"

I stared at her in amazement, for truly the thought of doing such a thing had never even crossed my mind; looking back, after months with the thermometer as necessary as a knife or a saucepan, I can hardly believe this to be possible, but so it was. To do myself justice, I recognized at once the brilliance of her suggestion, and would have acted on it at once had I had a thermometer. Neither of us, however, possessed one and as it was after closing time, I had to go all the way to John Bell and Croydon's all-night department to buy one, and when I got back Octavia had gone to sleep for the night and it didn't seem worth waking her. In the morning, however, I managed to take it and found that it was high, though not very high for a baby, but nevertheless high enough to justify ringing the doctor. To my surprise, the secretary girl did not sound at all put out when I asked if he could call, but seemed to take such a request for granted: I think I had half expected a lecture on my idleness and pretensions.

He arrived in the middle of the morning, and looked at her, and took her pulse, and took her temperature, and told me that it was nothing serious, in fact nothing at all, and then said if I didn't mind he ought to have a listen to her chest, so I pulled up her vest, and she smiled and wriggled with delight as he put the stethoscope on her fat ribs. He listened to her for a long time and I, who was beginning to think that perhaps I ought not to have bothered him after all, though it didn't seem to matter either way, sat there somewhat absently thinking how sweet she looked and that her vest could do with a wash. Had I known, I would have enjoyed that moment more, or perhaps I mean that I did enjoy that moment, and none since. For when he had finished listening to her, he stood up and took a deep breath and said, "Well, I don't think there's anything very much to worry about there."

"Oh, good," I said, already faint, for I could see he had not finished, and did not mean what he had said.

"Just the same," he said, "perhaps I ought to book you an appointment to take her along to the hospital."

"Oh," I said. This time I did not dare to ask, thinking of bad things like bronchial pneumonia, but of nothing bad enough, it seemed, which perhaps shows that even I am not naturally quick to accept ill news.

He was silent for a moment, expecting me to question him, I suppose, but I sat there with the child on my knee and said nothing. So after a while he said, no longer even pretending that there was nothing very much to worry about.

"It may well mean nothing at all, nothing at all. Where was she born? St. Andrew's, wasn't it? I can't believe they can have overlooked it. Perhaps the best thing would be for me to make you an appointment to go back there and see Protheroe, he's the man who would deal with this kind of thing."

"What is it?" I said at last. "What is it? Is it her chest? Is it pneumonia?"

"Oh, no," he said, "oh, no, nothing like that, nothing to do with this cold at all, the cold is nothing at all, every child in the neighbourhood's got that cold. It's just that I happened to hear something else while I was listening for it, that's all. It probably means nothing at all, nothing at all."

I suppose that most people would have asked him what he meant, but I was too frightened. I think that the truth was the last thing I wanted to hear, and I cannot even now think back to it. I wanted him to go on and on telling me that it was nothing, nothing at all. That was all that I wanted to hear, as though on my own deathbed. I did not even want him to tell me when the appointment would be for, as I was afraid it would be urgent, for that evening, for the next day, and when he started to tell me I tried not to listen, but I heard his voice coming to me, saying that it would probably be for the following week, for the following Thursday afternoon, but that he would let me know when he had confirmed it. I was relieved a little; he could not be expecting her to die before next Thursday. I even gathered enough strength to ask what I should do about her cold, and was not dismayed when he said nothing, nothing at all, except for a baby aspirin at night.

When he had gone, I went back and picked Octavia up and sat her on my knee and gazed at her, possessed by the most fearful anguish, aware, as all must be on such occasions, that my state had changed in ten minutes from unknown bliss to known though undefined sorrow. I wept, naturally, for I weep daily for some cause or other, and Octavia smiled at my tears and put her finger in them as they rolled down my cheek, as though they were raindrops on a window pane. It seemed that in comparison with this moment, the whole of my former life had been a summer afternoon. And yet, presumably, nothing was changed; in that instant of listening nothing had happened, except that ignorance had changed into knowledge. Often enough, over the next few weeks, I wished that I had remained ignorant, that I had never sent for the doctor and never found out. Peace of mind, fool's paradise, seemed to me at times to be better than profitable and useful misery, and it had never seemed that way to me before. They assure me I would have found out in the end, but I might have had a month more at least of ignorant delight. Though what difference would it have made? A month, a week, a day, an hour. It made quite a good deal of difference, in the event, but then I was not to know.

I really cannot look back upon that week. I had thought myself unhappy as a child, obsessed by unreal terrors, guilts and alarms, and as an adolescent, obsessed by myself, and as a woman, obsessed by the fear that my whole life and career were to be thrown into endless gloom by an evening's affection. But now for the first time I felt dread on another's behalf, and I found it insupportable. From time to time, stirring her soup in the pan, or clattering away at my typewriter in the BM typing room, I thought I would drop dead from the strain on my spirits. As I emerged from each fit of grief, I felt bitter resentment against Octavia and against the fate that had thus exposed me; up to this point, I had been thoroughly defended and protected against such onslaughts, but now I knew myself to be vulnerable, tender, naked, an easy target for the malice of chance. The fact that I was on my own, with no one to tell, made my anxiety both greater and more en-durable; for in the same instant in which I wished that I had someone, anyone, George, to weep at, I found myself glad that George had been spared this quite unnecessary sorrow.

I cannot bear to write about my first visit to hospital, that following week, though I feel some need to exorcise it. However, I cannot do so. It was intolerable. I waited, in a queue, with other small children and a sordid array of teddy bears and other rubbish, for an hour and a half; it was the time for her afternoon sleep, but she would never sleep on my knee, and she moaned and fretted and sucked her thumb and thrashed around till I was worn out from the effort of holding her. Then we saw the surgeon, and I did not dare to ask what he did not tell me, and then I had to trail her off to the X-ray department, a good mile away, it seemed, through dark corridors, and then back again to see the surgeon, who said something about the advisability of operating. This time I was in a trance, hardly listening to a word he was saying. Think about it, he said, and come back again the day after tomorrow. So we left, finally, two and a half hours after we had entered, and when we emerged from the hospital doors we were both crying bitterly, she from fatigue, and I from fatigue and fear.

We went home and I thought about it, and two days later I went back again and this time was not kept waiting more than twenty minutes, and was offered a cup of coffee by the surgeon when I got there. It seemed like charity to the condemned, but may not have been; it may just have been time for his coffee break. This time I was sufficiently hardened to notice his features, which before had been nothing but a dazzling blur, and to listen to what he was saying. He was murmuring gently on about the pulmonary artery; the very words were enough to throw me into a panic, so I stopped listening, for I could see that he was not really attempting to explain. When he had finished, and I had finished my burned institution coffee, he said, "So I think it would be advisable to operate as soon as possible."

"But you said," I said, remembering as though in a dream some other part of his conversation, "that it wasn't advisable to operate before the age of five or six."

"I was trying to explain to you," he said, "that we have really no choice. The severity of the condition varies so . . ."

"But there has been no sign of anything," I cried, suddenly coming round. "No sign. No symptoms. Nothing. She's always been so well."

"As I was saying," he said, "certain symptoms are not in

any case likely to become manifest until the child becomes more active. It was really a stroke of extraordinary luck that we discovered it at this stage, in view of the fact that there have been so few indications . . ."

"Luck, you call it, luck," I said, unable not to speak. "Luck, is it?" It has never ceased to amaze me that they showed, at this stage, so little professional sympathy; I see now, and suspected then, that his only emotion was professional curiosity. She was an odd case, my baby, a freak.

"Perhaps you could tell me," I said finally, when this retort received no response, and in a voice of renewed humility, "what the chances are. What per cent success you have."

"You must remember," he said, "that this kind of surgery is still in its very early stages, though we have been making great progress in the last few years. As little as five years ago, in an infant of this age, I should have said that the chance of survival was about five to one. Now we would put it at four to one, I think."

I almost think he expected me to congratulate him, but instead I burst into tears. It was the first time anyone had used the word survival to me, so bluntly.

"And otherwise," I said. "Otherwise, what would happen?"

"I am afraid," he said, "that there is no real alternative." And then, looking mildly concerned, he rose to his feet and said, "Now then, Mrs. Stacey, I think you'd better go home and talk it over with your husband, and do remember that we have every confidence . . ."

"Talk it over with who?" I said, ungrammatically, crossly, teetering on the edge of my self-control.

"Oh yes, of course, my goodness me," he said, looking back at his pile of documents. "But you do have someone you can discuss it with, surely? Your parents? Some relatives, surely?"

"My parents are in Africa," I said, standing up and buttoning up my coat, ready to go.

"In Africa?" He looked strangely interested by this piece of information, which I had volunteered in a spirit of defiance rather than of helpfulness; he sat down again and did a little thinking, and then looked up and said:

"You're not related to Herbert Stacey, are you?"

"As a matter of fact, I'm his daughter," I said grudgingly, aware that my avowal in these circumstances did my father little credit: but a change immediately passed over the whole demeanour of this man, who made me sit down once more and rang for another cup of coffee, and started to tell me how he was at Oxford with my father, and how they had belonged to this and that together, and spoken at this debate and that debate, and how he had always thought he would go in for politics, and how was my mother, and how were they finding Africa? Clearly, from his conversation, he had known both my parents quite well, and indeed, now I came to think of it, his name, which was Protheroe, was a name I had heard bandied around the dinner table a good deal at one time, and with favourable mention, too, for he was on the right side about the Health Service, and sufficiently distinguished to make distinguished remarks about it at conferences. A good socialist, this man was said to be, and we looked at each other with renewed interest.

We chatted amiably for at least a quarter of an hour more, during which time all the other wretched patients doubtless piled up in the waiting rooms outside with weary resignation; when he finally rose to let me go, he shook my hand warmly, took my telephone number, and said that I could bring the baby in for observation for a day in about a week's time, and that they would probably operate, all being well, in about a fortnight.

"Believe me," he said, "I won't pretend it isn't a big job, but she does seem to be unusually well despite her condition, and the chances of recovery, once we get past the initial stages, are excellent, quite excellent. And believe me, Miss Stacey, though I say it myself, she's in good hands here, you couldn't get her anywhere better."

And I believed him, too. Although I had never doubted his competence, I felt happier when he asserted it with a smile in this way. Flesh is weak, and we ask for too much, but it's a comfort when we get it, and without paying.

I did not know what to do with myself for the next fortnight: I was really off work, and consistently off, too, not just fancying I was off until I made myself open the books. I struggled through the days as best I could, tormented by Octavia's lovely smiling gaiety, and trying not to pick her up too often. Then, the second evening, it occurred to me that I needed a drink, so I took to drink. I think I have said elsewhere that drink always cheers me up, and it even managed to cheer me now. Being rather hard up, I bought very cheap red wine, which I quite liked if I warmed it up in a saucepan first. I drank a lot each evening, and after an hour or so reached a state where my thoughts swam dizzily from one optimistic refuge to another: one moment convinced of the immortality of the soul, the next that no pain is without purpose, but basically, quite simply sure, as I never am when sober, that luck and the odds were on my side.

Most nights I was in bed before Lydia got in, as her affair with Joe was at this time at its height. I tried to avoid her, deliberately, as I had not imparted the truth about Octavia, and did not wish to be trapped into doing so. One evening, though, she and Joe came back together just after eleven while I was lying on the hearth rug with my head on a cushion, wondering if I had the energy to get up and go to bed. I did not hear them coming and they discovered me there. They noticed at once the evidence that I had been drinking, and decided to join me. They told me about the film they had been to see that evening at the Cameo-Poly, and Lydia said that she had just about finished her novel, and I asked Joe about his, and he said which, and I said whichever one he was writing, and he said he wasn't, and I said *that* was a change. Then he started on about when were my parents coming home, and when would Lydia have to move out, and what was I going to do for a flat, it must be difficult finding one with a baby. Whereupon a sudden faintness seized me, for I knew with piercing premonition exactly what everyone would say if Octavia were to die. They would say it was a blessing in disguise. I could hear them saying it, even those who knew and understood me, for apart from myself there was nobody in the world who cared about her, or who realized that I cared. Perhaps there are some for whom no one cares, deserted, abandoned, unloved, unwanted, whose existence is a needless burden to the earth they lie upon. Perhaps I was obliged to make up for what Octavia lacked in quantity of mourners by the quality of my caring.

Luckily, they soon passed from the subject of flats and babies, and I was able to recover myself, though only momentarily, for what Joe said very shortly was "I was talking about you, Rosamund, the other night, to that friend of yours from the BBC. George he's called, isn't he? George what? I can never think of his other name."

"George Matthews," I said. "George Matthews, you mean."

"That's right," said Joe. "George Matthews."

There was a following silence, in which I registered the loud beating of my heart, the sudden burning of my face, and some weird interruptions of my breathing, which indicated the extent of my concern. It was months since I had even heard his name, for I had not even had the privilege, so often enjoyed by other unrequited lovers, of hearing his character and affairs discussed by friends; I had so sedulously avoided any vague connections that he might well have never existed, and indeed, had I not held the fruit of his existence so often in my arms, I would have thought the whole episode nothing but a dream, begotten from some strange frustrated quirk within myself, some wishful dream of what might have taken place. Now that at last I heard him mentioned, now that he emerged at last from the private recesses of my memory, I did not know what to say, nor how to behave with any semblance of flippancy. There were a hundred things that I wanted to ask; what he looked like, what he was wearing, whether he had recalled me with tenderness, indifference or hostility, whether he had known about my baby, whom he had been with, who loved him, whom did he love, a hundred questions like these, so long repressed and restrained, came at once into my head, but I could not think how to phrase them, so I said nothing. I said nothing, and I felt my face settle inexorably into its lines of habitual dismissive blankness. I must have convinced Joe of my total lack of interest, for when he looked up from stubbing out his cigarette he did not pursue the topic but continued instead to talk about his television program. Lydia was going to be on it, talking about the modern novel. "Why not, after all?" said Joe. "She's as much right to talk about the modern novel as anyone else, haven't you, Lydia? And she's pretty, too, so why not?"

Why not, indeed, I said to myself as I took myself to bed and left them to it. Why ever not? It seemed to me of no importance. I was sick of them, sick of hearing them and being with them and thinking about them. And yet I liked them. If I liked anyone, they were the kind of people I liked. I began to think that I did not like anyone any more. Except George, George with his quiet anonymity, George who could live within half a mile of me and remain for over a year unmentioned, unseen, receding endlessly out of recollection and out of my life. I thought I liked George. I wished I could have had an opportunity for telling him so.

The night before Octavia's operation I lay awake, enduring what might have been my last battle with the vast shadowy monsters of doubt. Some on such occasions must doubt the existence of God; it does not seem to me natural to survive such disasters with faith unimpaired. I find it more honourable to take events into consideration, when speaking of the mercy of God. But, in fact, the subject of God did not much cross my mind, for I had never given it much thought, having been brought up a good Fabian rationalist, and notions such as the afterlife and heaven seemed to me crude quite literally beyond belief. Justice, however, preoccupied me. I could not rid myself of the notion that if Octavia were to die, this would be a vengeance upon my sin. The innocent shall suffer for the guilty. What my sin had been I found difficult to determine, for I could not convince myself that sleeping with George had been a sin; on the contrary, in certain moods I tended to look on it as the only virtuous action of my life. A sense of retribution nevertheless hung heavily over me, and what I tried to preserve that night was faith not in God but in the laws of chance.

Towards morning, I began to think that my sin lay in my love for her. For five minutes or so, I almost hoped that she might die, and thus relieve me of the corruption and the fatality of love. Ben Jonson said of his dead child, my sin was too much hope of thee, loved boy. We too easily take what the poets write as figures of speech, as pretty images, as strings of *bons mots*. Sometimes perhaps they speak the truth.

In the morning, when it was time to get up and get dressed and gather together her pitiably small requirements, I got out of bed and got down on my knees and said, Oh God, let her survive, let her live, let her be all right, and God was created by my need, perhaps.

We went to the hospital and I handed her over, and she smiled at me, then cried when they took her away. The world had contracted to the small size of her face and her clenching, waving hands. The poignancy was intolerable: her innocence, her gaiety, her size. I went away, and I walked up and down Marylebone Road. I cannot think what I did with the hours. I did not go back till half an hour after they had told me to inquire, and when I got there I did not dare to ask. I stood there, waiting, till someone recognized me and came over smiling and told me that everything had gone extremely well, and that Mr. Protheroe sent his regards and hoped to see me, and that there was every hope of complete success. As on the day when I had first guessed at her condition, I could not believe that a mere recital of facts could thus change my fate: I stood there, dumbly, wondering if it could be the truth that she had told me, or whether she had got the wrong name, the wrong data, the wrong message. But she went on smiling and reassuring me, and soon I believed her, for it became suddenly clear that it was quite out of the question that anything should have gone wrong, that of course we had been lucky, Octavia and I. When I got round to speaking, I asked if I could see her, and they said to come back in the morning, as she was still unconscious and not to be disturbed. Of course, I said humbly, and backed away, full of gratitude towards the lot of them: then I went and wept copiously in the cloakroom, and then I went home.

It was only when I got home that I began to be preoccupied by certain details upon which I had not previously dared to exercise my mind. What would Octavia think when she woke in hospital? Would she be in terrible pain from the operation? Would they feed her properly? Would she cry? Earlier it had seemed presumptuous to have considered these things, but now their importance swelled minute by minute in my mind. The threat of fatality removed, the conditions of life at once resumed their old significance. It was the strangeness, I thought, more than the pain that would afflict her, for she liked nobody but me; even Mrs. Jennings and Lydia she regarded only with tolerance, and strangers she disliked with noisy vehemence. Lord knows what incommunicable small terrors infants go through, unknown to all. We disregard them, we say they forget, because they have not the words to make us remember, because they cannot torment our consciences with a recital of their woes. By the time they learn to speak they have forgotten the details of their complaints, and so we never know. They forget so quickly, we say, because we cannot contemplate the fact that they never forget. We cannot stand the injustice of life, so we pretend that a baby can forget hours spent wrapped in newspaper on the floor of a telephone kiosk, the vicious blows of the only ones that might have loved it, the sight of its elder, unsaved brothers in a blazing mass of oil-stove flames. Like Job's comforters, we cannot believe that the innocent suffer. And yet they do. We see, but we cannot believe.

When I went round in the morning to visit her, I found myself met by a certain unhelpful stalling. The lady in charge, a lady in white whose title was not clear to me, assured me that all was well, that all was progressing most satisfactorily, that the child was as comfortable as could be expected. "I'd like to go and see her," I said then, summoning up a little courage.

"I'm afraid that won't be possible," said the lady in white with calm certainty, looking down at her file of notes.

"Why not?" I said. "I would like to see her, I know she'd like to see me."

The lady in white embarked upon a long explanation about upsetting children, upsetting mothers, upsetting other children, upsetting other mothers, justice to all, disturbing the nurses' routine, and such topics. As she talked, in her smooth even tones, all kinds of memories filtered back into my mind, memories of correspondences in *The Times* and *The Guardian* upon this very subject, composed of letters from mothers like myself who had not been allowed in. "What about visiting hours?" I said, and back came the civil, predictable answer,

"I'm afraid that for such small infants we don't allow any visiting time at all. We really do find that it causes more inconvenience to staff and patients than we can possibly cope with. Really, Mrs. Stacey, you must understand that it is of no practical use to visit such a young child, she will settle much more happily if she doesn't see you. You'd be amazed to see how soon they settle down. Mothers never believe us, but we know from experience how right we are to make this regulation."

I didn't like the sound of that word "settle": it suggested a settling into lethargy and torpor, such as I remembered to have read of in *The Times*. Octavia had never been settled in her short life, and I did not want her to begin now. Already, in twenty-four hours, we had endured the longest separation of our lives, and I began to see it stretching away, indefinitely prolonged. Also, because they would not let me see the child, I suspected that they had not told me the whole truth about her recovery; was there now in her small countenance something too dreadful for me to behold? I voiced this fear, feeling that it would have effect, and be at least appreciated.

"I can't believe until I see her," I said, "that everything really is all right. I just can't believe it."

She took my point. "Mrs. Stacey," she said, looking up and meeting with straight, woman-to-woman frankness my anxious gaze, "you must believe me when I say that I have given you all the information there is about your daughter. We are making no attempt to conceal anything from you because there is nothing to conceal. Mr. Protheroe expressed personal satisfaction at the progress of the operation and is calling in this morning to check on progress. If you would like to see his report, here it is."

And she detached a piece of paper from the file marked Not To Be Seen By Patient and pushed it over to me. I glanced at it, but could see it was nothing but a mass of technicalities, so I did not try to read it. I felt better, though, by virtue of the fact that she had let me look, for she could not reasonably have relied upon the exact extent of my ignorance. By this time it was quite easy to tell from her expression that she considered I was nothing but an ordinary and tedious time-waster, and as I dislike being any such thing, and as I could see that I was making no progress, I decided that I had no choice but to leave gracefully, so I did.

"Oh well," I said, "perhaps you're right. I'm sure you're looking after her properly; it was just that I wanted to see her, I thought she might be missing me. But perhaps you're right, perhaps it wouldn't do any good to see her so soon."

And I picked up my bag and prepared to go. She got up from behind her desk and opened the door for me; I was out in the corridor before I heard her saying that perhaps in a fortnight or so I might be able to visit. I half turned to retort, but had not the energy, so I continued on down the corridor and out of the building. I knew my way round that place now as well as if it were my school or my college or the British Museum itself.

I had not expected that they would let me stay with her all day, and had arrived prepared to go on to the BM to work, intending to call back at teatime. I went on to the BM mechanically, and spent an hour or two there trying to check up on some very insignificant footnotes, but it was not the kind of work that could occupy the mind, and by lunchtime I had had enough. My thesis was so nearly finished that I anyway somewhat disliked the prospect of its final completion and all the rethinking and restarting on new projects that it would entail. I went downstairs for a sandwich and a coffee, and while there sat quietly and told myself that I should be grateful, that I should not now be worrying about not seeing my child for a fortnight, that regulations were regulations, that I should be grateful and should not obstruct. But the more I told myself all this, the less I convinced myself, for I had only to think of my baby's small lonely awakening for the whole pack of thoughts to seem so much waste irrelevant rubbish. And when I had finished my coffee, I got up and put my books back in my bag and went back to the hospital.

It was lunchtime and I could not find the lady in white. There were a couple of nurses guarding her office, who said she would not be back till two.

"That doesn't matter," I said. "It wasn't her I wanted to see, it was my baby. Would one of you take me to see my baby? She's in ward 21G. Octavia Stacey, her name is."

The two nurses looked at each other, nervously, as though I were a case.

"You're not allowed to visit in this ward," one of them said, with timid politeness, propitiating, kind, as one speaks to the sick or the mad.

"I don't really care," I said, "whether I'm allowed to visit or not. If you'll tell me where it is, I'll get there by myself, and you needn't even say you saw me."

"I'm afraid we can't possibly do that," the other one said when the first speaker said nothing. Like her friend, she had a timid, undetermined note in her voice, and I felt mean to pursue my point. I did pursue it, however; I told them I had no intention of not seeing my baby, that I didn't think it would upset her at all, but that on the contrary it would cheer her up, and cheer me up, and was in every way desirable, and that if they didn't tell me how to find her I would just go and look for myself. No, no, I couldn't possibly do that, they both said at once, their voices hardening from personal timidity and embarrassment into the weight of authority. They had that whole building behind them, they knew, and I had nothing behind me at all except my intention. I have never been good at getting what I want; every impulse in me tells me to give up at the first breath of opposition. And yet this time I felt that I would not be the only one to lose; somewhere Octavia was lying around and waiting for me. It was no longer a question of what I wanted: this time there was someone else involved. Life would never be a simple question of self-denial again.

"I must see her," I repeated. "If you won't let me go, go and get Sister, or Matron, or whatever she's called. Go and fetch her for me. Or I'll wait here till she comes."

"She won't be here till two," said one, and the other said, "You can't wait here, you aren't allowed to wait."

"What do you mean, I'm not allowed?" I said crossly, suffering greatly from this as yet mild degree of self-assertion. "Who doesn't allow me? Who says I can't wait?"

"Sister won't see anyone anyway, at this time of day," they said. "And she says that no one must be allowed to wait."

They began to look frightened; I could see they were going to get into trouble if I were still there when Sister came back. I was sorry for them, but not as sorry as I was for Octavia. I sat down on the desk and I waited. After five minutes one of them disappeared, perhaps in an effort to find someone more persuasive to dislodge me, but before she returned Sister arrived, and the remaining girl had to bear the brunt of her wrath.

"Well, well, Mrs. Stacey," she said snappily as she bustled in. "So you're here again, are you? Now then, Miss Richards, how many times have I told you this isn't a convenient time for visitors? Mrs. Stacey, I'm afraid that I can't possibly talk . . ."

"I'm not supposed to be on duty now," said Miss Richards querulously, interrupting. "I was only here because of Mavis, and then Mavis went off to look for . . ."

"I don't care who went off where," said Sister, fiercely, "I have said again and again that my office must not be used as a waiting room. Mrs. Stacey, I'm afraid I am far too busy to talk to you now. Miss Richards, would you show Mrs. Stacey to the lift, please. If there is anything you wish to discuss, you must..."

"I don't want to discuss anything," I said. "I've come to visit my baby."

I felt happier now; I had not enjoyed upsetting those unimpressive nurses, whose discomfort in the situation had been almost as great as mine. In Sister, however, I sensed the kind of will that can be fought: she found pleasure, not torment, in assertion, so I felt free to assert myself too.

"I told you this morning," said Sister, "that visiting is quite out of the question."

"I don't care what you told me," I said. "I want to see my baby. If you don't take me straight there, I shall walk round until I find the way myself. She's not kept under lock and key, I assume?"

"Mrs. Stacey," said Sister, "you are behaving most foolishly, and I must ask you to leave at once."

"I won't leave," I said. "You'd much better take me straight there, I don't want to be compelled to wander round upsetting the whole of your hospital until I find my baby."

"Now then, now then," said Sister, "this is neither the time nor the place for hysterical talk like that. We must all be grateful that your child is..."

"Grateful," I said. "I am grateful. I admire your hospital, I admire your work, I am devoted to the National Health Service. Now I want to see my baby."

She came over to me and took my arm and started to push me gently towards the door; I have spent so much of my life in intelligent, superior effort to understand ignorance that I recognized her look at once. She pitied me and she was amazed. I let her get me as far as the door, being unable at first to resist the physical sense of propulsion, but when we got to the door I stopped and said, "No, I'm not going to leave. I'm going to stay here until you change your mind."

"I have no intention of changing my mind," she said, and once more took hold of my elbow and started to push. I resisted. We stood there for a moment; I could not believe that physical violence could possibly take place, but on the other hand I did not see what else I could do. So when she started to push, I started to scream. I screamed very loudly, shutting my eyes to do it, and listening in amazement to the deafening shindy that filled my head. Once I had started, I could not stop; I stood there, motionless, screaming, whilst they shook me and yelled at me and told me that I was upsetting everybody in earshot. "I don't care," I yelled, finding words for my inarticulate passion, "I don't care, I don't care, I don't care about anyone, I don't care, I don't care, I don't care."

Eventually they got me to sit down, but I went on screaming and moaning and keeping my eyes shut; through the noise I could hear things happening, people coming and going, someone slapped my face, someone tried to put a wet flannel on my head, and all the time I was thinking I must go on doing this until they let me see her. Inside my head it was red and black and very hot, I remember, and I remember also the clearness of my consciousness and the ferocity of my emotion, and myself enduring them, myself neither one nor the other, but enduring them, and not breaking in two. After a while I heard someone shouting above the din, "For God's sake tell her she can see the baby, someone try and tell her," and I heard these words and instantly stopped and opened my eyes and beheld the stricken, confused silence around me.

"Did you say I could see the baby?" I said.

"Of course you can see the baby," said Mr. Protheroe. "Of course you can see the baby. I cannot imagine why you should have ever been prevented from seeing the baby."

I looked at the breathless circle surrounding me, which had changed its composition considerably since I had last seen it: Mr. Protheroe himself looked agitated and white with anger, Sister was sitting in a corner and crying into a handkerchief, the nurses were looking stunned, and there were a couple more men also looking angry. It was as though I had opened my eyes on a whole narrative caught in a single picture, a narrative in which I myself had taken no part; it had been played out between the Sister and the others, quite clearly, and she had lost and was now suffering her defeat. It was nothing to do with me at all, I felt; I shut my eyes, wearily, upon them, for I did not want to know. I had no interest in their story; I wished to know only my own. I felt I could no longer bother to endure their conflicts; if I had gained my point, that was enough for me.

"Can I go now and see my baby?" I asked.

"I will take you myself," said Mr. Protheroe, and I got up, and he took my arm and conducted me down the corridor. To my surprise I found that I needed his arm, for my knees were weak and the blood was singing in my ears, sensations odd enough for one who had always looked and felt as strong as a horse, as my parents used to say. We went along various devious passages, through swing doors and up and down half-flights of stairs, while I tried in vain to memorize the route, like Theseus in the labyrinth, and finally emerged in a long, cubicled ward full of small children. The cubicles must have been soundproofed, for when we reached Octavia I heard nothing until they opened the door, and at once her sad, piercing and recognizable wails met my ear. She was lying there on a cot much like the one in which she had spent the first days of her life, and wearing the same kind of institution nightie, but this time she was strapped in. I stood on the threshold, overcome with feeling, and she turned her eyes towards me, and I was afraid she would weep all the more bitterly, or fail to recognize me at all, but instead she stopped crying, and I went up to her, and her face became suffused with its habitual enchanted and enchanting total smile. She lay there smiling, unable to move but smiling, and I went up to her and stroked her cheek and she smiled more and more. She had forgiven me for our day of separation, I could see, and such generosity I found amazing, for I am not generous. Fair, but not generous.

I stayed with her all day, and helped to feed her, and watched her sleep and watched her wake and watched her cry, for she did cry, but through restless boredom and pain, not through desertion. Mr. Protheroe, who had had to leave me after five minutes, had said that they were to find me a chair, and let me in any day I wished to come, and that I could eat in the canteen. I asked him, when no one was there, whether this was preferential treatment, and whether I was receiving it because I made such a fuss, or because he had known my father: he said that it was not preferential treatment, the policy of the hospital was to admit mothers with children, the policy of the nation was to admit mothers with children, but that nevertheless the human element intervened. "Our buildings here are old," he said, "and our staff are old. We have to put up with it." "Admit it, though," I said. "I only got in because I made a fuss. Other mothers don't get in, do they?"

"They don't all want to," he said. "They don't all have time to. Some of them have families at home to worry about. I wouldn't think about the others, if I were you. Think about yourself."

So I did think about myself and I went on coming, regardless of all the others who couldn't come. They did not like me to be there, most of them, and they never found me a chair, but I wasn't bothered about a chair, and when I could not find one for myself I sat on the floor. It was quite peaceful, as she slept much of the time, so I was able to read and get bored in a fairly normal fashion. Sister Watkins would not speak to me, so deep was her resentment for what she had endured through my innocent agency, but the twinges of guilt that I felt whenever I encountered her were fainter than any I can recollect. Towards the end, however, try as I would, I could no longer stifle awareness of the other small ones, crying quietly and unheard behind their glass doors, or lying in a stupor of nothingness at the other end of the long ward, unprotected by partitions. There were only very small children in that part of the hospital; I did manage to see some larger ones, on one of my detours to the canteen, and some of them looked much better, and were reading and playing and shouting at each other. I saw some terrible sights, and even from time to time indulged the dreadful fancy that I was glad that Octavia's illness, however grave, had in no way marred her beauty. But this was but a fancy, for who would not rather endure a hare lip? Before Octavia was born, I used to think that love bore some relation to merit and to beauty, but now I saw that this was not so.

It must have been the saddest place in the world, that hospital. The decor made faint attempts at cheer, for there were friezes of bunny rabbits round the walls, and from time to time one particularly enthusiastic nurse would come and talk to me and dangle teddy bears at Octavia. Octavia took no interest in teddy bears, being at an age where she would play only with hard chewable objects or paper, but the nurse did not notice. I seemed to spend weeks there, for she was in for a long time, and during those weeks I saw only one other mother; we met, twice, at the entrance to the ward, and the second time accompanied each other more or less accidentally down to the canteen, where we sat, after brief and watery smiles, at the same table with our cups of tea. There seemed little small talk in which one could indulge, for any however trivial inquiry might well in those circumstances let loose unwelcome, dormant fear and tragedy, so finally all I said was, "How did you manage to get in?" I wanted to talk to her, for she looked a nice woman; older than myself, with fair

hair parted in the middle and draped looping gently back-
wards, and wearing a belted grey coat with a fur collar.
Her face was one of those mild, round-chinned, long-
cheeked faces, without angles or edges, but nevertheless
shapely and memorable, with a kind of soft tranquillity.
She looked, too, as if she could talk, and I had had enough
of my endless battle with the official and the inarticulate.

"Oh, I got in all right," she said. "I made them give it
me in writing before I let him in, that I could come. Then
all one has to do is show them the letter."

"That shows foresight," I said. "I had to have hysterics."

"Really?" she smiled, impressed. "And it worked, did
it?"

"Evidently."

"I was always afraid," she said, "that if I made a real
fuss, they wouldn't let me in anyway, because they'd say I
was in too bad a state to see the children. I was afraid
they'd put me to bed, too."

I thought that this might well have been more than
likely in my case too, and I thought about what Lydia had
said about not being allowed to have an abortion because
it would upset her; degrees of madness were a tricky matter, it seemed, as were degrees of responsibility.

"Anyway," I said, "you didn't have to make a fuss. You
did it all properly. I didn't realize what it would be like; if
I'd realized I would have done something about it earlier
too, perhaps."

"One doesn't realize," she said. "The first time, I'd no
idea. They wouldn't let me in with the first child. I had to
get my husband to write a letter."

"And that worked?"

"Oh yes. My husband has some influence here, you see.
Some. I don't know what one would do without a little
influence." She smiled, wanly, and I noticed that she
looked very, very tired.

"But how many children?" I asked. "More than one child?"

"It's my second," she said, "that's in now. My second boy."

There was a pause; she expected me to ask her what was wrong, perhaps, but I did not like to, and I could see that she was relieved by my abstention, for she went on, "It's the same thing with both of them. So I knew it was coming this time, I've known for years. It makes it worse. People think it makes it better, but it makes it worse."

"Why did you let him come here, after the other one?"

"Why? It's the best place, you know. They must have told you it's the best place."

"Oh yes, they did. But I thought they said that everywhere."

She smiled once more, her grave slow liquid smile, a smile not of amusement but of tired well-meaning. "Oh no," she said, "it really is. You're very lucky. They really are wonderful here. It's your first, isn't it?"

"Yes, my first."

"I wish you luck," she said, finishing her cup of tea, "with your second."

"I'm not having any more," I said.

"That's what I said," she said. "They said it wasn't likely to happen twice. And afterwards they told me the odds. Not that it matters. I'd have done it anyway."

"But how," I said, "how do you bear it?" I did not mean to say it, but I said it in spite of myself and then wished I had not spoken, for her manner, though kind, had been impersonal, a sort of cool human sympathy rather than a personal interest. She did not mind, however; she seemed used to the question.

"I don't bear it," she said. She picked up her spoon and started to stir the leaves in the bottom of her cup, staring at them intently as though fate were indeed lying there amongst them, sodden and dark brown, to be altered by the movement of a tin spoon. "At first I used to pretend not to mind, I used to laugh it off to my friends and underestimate its gravity when talking to my family, you know what I mean. Extraordinary, the impulse to play things down, don't you think? But in the end I got fed up with it. I got tired of pretending it was nothing just to save other people's feelings. Now I don't care who sees I care."

She stopped talking as though she had said all she had to say. I too said nothing, awed by this testimony of long-term sorrow. There was still something in me that protested, that told me that it was not possible that a mere accident of birth, the slight misjudgment of part of one organ should so mould and pin and clamp a nature that it could grow like this, warped and graceful, up the one sunny wall of dignity left to it. For, no doubt about it, she wore her grief well: she spared herself and her associates the additional infliction of ugliness, which so often accompanies much pain.

We sat there for a moment or two, quietly, and I meant to say no more, but after a while my nature returned, relentless, to its preoccupations, like a dog to some old dried marrowless bone. I could not help but ask; I had no hope of an answer, having always known that there is no answer, but it seemed to me that this woman would at least understand the terms of my question.

"What," I said to her then, "what about all the others?"

"The others?" she said slowly.

"The others," I said. "Those that don't even get in. Those without money. Those without influence. Those who would not dare to have hysterics."

"Ah, those," she said.

"Yes, those. What about them?"

"I don't know," she said, still speaking slowly, her eyes still downcast. "I don't know. I can't see that I can do anything about them."

"But don't they worry you?" I said, reluctant to disturb her yet unable to desist.

With difficulty she began to attach herself to the question. She began to speak, and I waited with ridiculous expectation for her answer.

"They used to worry me," she said. "When I first started on all this, they worried me almost as much as my own. And I comforted myself by saying that nobody felt what I felt. They don't care, I said, or they would do what I do. But that's not true, of course."

She looked at me for confirmation, and I nodded, for I agreed with what she had said.

"They do care," she went on, "but they don't set about it as I do. As time went on, though, and after years of this, I began to think that it was after all nothing to do with me. And it isn't, you know. My concerns are my concerns, and that's where it ends. I haven't the energy to go worrying about other people's children. They're nothing to do with me. I only have enough time to worry about myself. If I didn't put myself and mine first, they wouldn't survive. So I put them first and the others can look after themselves."

She finished speaking; she had no more to say. I was, inevitably, touched almost to tears, for it is very rare that one meets someone who will give one such an answer to my question. She had spoken without harshness; I think it was that that had touched me most. I had so often heard these views expressed, but always before they had been accompanied by a guilty sneer at those who must be neglected, or a brisk Tory contempt for the ignorant, or a business-like blinkered air of proud realism. I had never heard them thus gently put forward as the result of sad necessity. I saw what she meant; I saw, in her, what all the others meant. I don't think I replied, and after a while she put on her gloves and stood up.

"Good-bye," she said.

"Good-bye," I said. And she went.

It was about a week later that I was able to take Octavia home. She was by this time quite gay and mobile once more, and seemingly unaffected, apart from loss of weight, by her ordeal. I arrived on the morning of her release with a small suitcase full of real clothes for her to wear; I had been looking forward to dressing her in something other than the white institutional nighties the hospital provided. In fact, I had whiled away some of my vigil by her cotside by making her some new dresses; I had been taught at school to smock, an accomplishment I had never thought to use, but I do not like to let anything be wasted, and I had made her some very pretty small garments in various dark smart shades of Viyella. It had given me much satisfaction to make them; it was more profitable than jigsaws, for it actually saved money, while at the same time gratifying the need to do something mechanical with my hands, which otherwise occupied themselves by ripping holes in my cuticles or tearing strips off the wicker-seated chair I had finally acquired. I put her in my masterpiece to take her home: it was dark blue with a very small check. She looked very charming in it and jumped happily on my knee. I shook hands with all the nurses and even with Sister, who was glad to see me go. I got into the waiting taxi and off we went: I remembered the last time she and I had left the place together in this way, when she had been ten days old. I now knew better than to hope I would never have to go back again, for I knew that at the best she and I were in for a lifetime of checks and examinations, but nevertheless it seemed to me that I was more happy and more fortunate now than I had been then.

It was the middle of the afternoon: owing to the curious nature of the one-way street system, the quickest way to approach the flat was to go round Queens Crescent and then to the right off Portland Place. The air was bright and clear, and as we drove past the formal determined structure of the Crescent, ever-demolished, ever-renewed, I suddenly thought that perhaps I could take it and survive. I had thought this before when drunk but never when sober; up till that moment I had been inwardly convinced that too much worry would rot my nature beyond any hope of fruit or even of flower. But then, however fleetingly, I felt that I could take what I had been given to take. I felt, for the first time since Octavia's birth, a sense of adequacy. Like Job, I had been threatened with the worst and, like Job, I had kept my shape. I knew something now of the quality of life, and anything in the way of happiness that I should hereafter receive would be based on fact and not on hope.

When we got back home and settled in, Octavia and I, I found that my initial relief was quickly replaced by new anxieties. I had foreseen this, so was not alarmed or taken by surprise; but nevertheless, it would have been nice to have had a little time off. Now that I was no longer concerned by immediate life or death, the minor details of health began to obsess me: I had been warned that it would be dangerous for the baby to contract the most insignificant ailments, and that any cold or scratch must be instantly counteracted by penicillin. Consequently, I spent my time watching her anxiously and hardly dared to leave her to the care of Mrs. Jennings, despite her eagerness to have her. All the normal preoccupations of motherhood were in me hideously enlarged, and I dreamed of them at nights.

I also began to worry about where I would live when my parents got back. They wrote to me about once a month, and when they wrote they always made vague references to being back for Christmas: not knowing my situation, they clearly did not think it necessary to go into any detail. I had made no plans: it was not in me to tempt fate by arranging in advance accommodation for myself and a child who might well not exist, who might well by Christmas have been as though she had never existed. Now, though, it seemed that she was going to go on being there, and that I would not be able to present my parents with a desolate flat, carefully emptied of all nappies, bootees, plastic ducks and orange-juice bottles. The other possibility was that I should not move. I could always have stayed there and faced them, and asked if I could go on living there. There would have been room and they would have said Yes. But it was not in my nature to ask favours, and anyway I would not have liked to live with them, despite the advantages. Without the flat, my economic situation would be grave: when I got Octavia home, I made a gesture towards action by writing off to all my friends on magazines, to the firm of tutors I had taught for, and to various educational agencies, in search of extra work.

As it turned out, I need not have bothered. At the end of the first week of December I had a letter from my father, saying that they had decided to go to India for the year, at the invitation of the government. "Being so near anyway," he wrote, "I thought that we might as well continue on our way, without the expense of a return journey. We shall be sorry, of course, not to see you and Beatrice and the children, but you all sound very busy and happy, and can do quite well without us, I am sure." As I read this, I was overcome with relief at the unexpected reprieve. I had a whole year's grace, and who knows what might have happened at the end of a year? For one thing, my thesis would be finished and published, and with any luck I would have a reputable university appointment to confront them with by the autumn, as well as a small baby. I continued the letter, overcome with unashamed relief; my father went on to speak of his work in Africa, of various problems they had encountered, of the climate, and then, quite casually, in the last paragraph, the last sentence even, he said, "I had a letter from our old friend Dick

Protheroe last week, who says he has been seeing something of you." Nothing more: just that. After this all-revealing remark, he quietly signed himself off in his usual manner; yours ever, Papa.

I sat and looked at the letter for some time, pursuing its implications. It was quite clear to me, as it might not have been to others, that Mr. Protheroe had told my parents the whole story of Octavia's existence, and of her illness, and that by this apparently chance remark my father had meant to let me know that he knew. There was nothing amazing in itself in the fact that they had found out: news reaches even Africa, and sooner or later they would have got to know. I was more surprised, in a sense, that they had remained in the dark for so long: it proved that neither Beatrice nor Clare had told on me. Beatrice's reticence did not surprise me, as it is an ineradicable family trait, but I had had my suspicions about Clare and also about various stray acquaintances whom I had glimpsed from time to time in passing cars and in cinema queues. However, it had been left to Mr. Protheroe, who had considered it honourable to inform on me.

When I looked at the consequences of his information, I could not find it in me to regret it. For, extraordinary as it may seem, I was and am convinced that my parents decided to go to India and to refrain from revisiting England largely because they did not want to upset me and my domestic arrangements. I can see, objectively, how extraordinary it is to read such mighty meanings into what my father wrote, but nevertheless, knowing my parents, I am sure that I was right. They did not wish to cause me or themselves pain, embarrassment, or even mere inconvenience by their return, so they went to India instead. I think, too, that they wished me to understand this, or they would have gone, just gone, without mentioning Protheroe's name. His name was there to give me the terms of their departure: perhaps as the mildest of reproaches, but more likely as an indication of the seriousness of their intent. Their behaviour seemed natural to me, for I am their child, but I have speculated endlessly about whether or not they were right. Such tact, such withdrawal, such avoidance. Such fear of causing pain, such willingness to receive and take pains. It is a morality, all right, a well-established, traditional, English morality, moreover it is my morality, whether I like it or not. But there are things in me that cannot take it, and when they have to assert themselves the result is violence, screaming, ugliness, and Lord knows what yet to come.

As a child, I used to endure any discomfort rather than cause offense. I would eat things I loathed, freeze to death in underheated sitting rooms, roast under hair dryers, drink in cafés from chipped and filthy cups, rather than offend hosts, waitresses, hairdressers. To me the pain of causing trouble was greater than anything that I myself within myself could endure. But as I grow older, I find myself changing a little. Partly it is because, with Octavia, I cannot inflict all hardship on myself alone: what I take for myself, she gets too. And so I was glad that my parents went to India; the physical comfort of their absence was greater to me than the mental disquiet of considering that they had taken so large a decision on my account. There was a time when this would not have been so; I sat at the kitchen table with the letter still open in front of me, and contemplated my growing selfishness, and thought that this was probably maturity. My parents are still children, maybe: they think that they can remain innocent. Or that is one way of looking at it. From another point of view, a more warm and fleshly point, they are perhaps as dangerous and cruel as that father in Washington Square.

I told Octavia the good news, and she smiled and waved at me from her high chair, and offered me a small wet piece of rusk as a reciprocal effort at communication. When I declined it, she dropped it on the floor, and I thought with relief that I had at least another year to clear up the mess and squalor that she had inflicted on the once elegant flat. I got her out of the chair, and put her to crawl along the corridor while I went to see if Lydia was in; I had not heard her come in the night before, but if she was in I wanted to tell her about what my father had said, and to discuss its moral quality with her. I knocked on her door and there was no answer; as it was past ten, I pushed it open to see if she was there, which she was not. I went back to the kitchen and did a little washing and tidying up, and then went into the sitting room and got out my typewriter to write a review of a book on Daniel Defoe for a very unimportant magazine. It was a task for which I was ill-equipped, and not a very profitable task at that, if one takes hours per pound into consideration, for to review this one book I had felt it necessary to read the works of Defoe himself. Such was my ignorance of the man that I had managed to read the whole of the *Journal of the Plague Year* without realizing that it was a fictional and not a factual account of the horrible events, which says much for Defoe but little for me. I was extremely put out when I found that it wasn't, as they say, true, and even more put out that I was put out, as I have always maintained that I hold an Aristotelian and not a Platonic view of fact and fiction. I had just written and counted my first hundred words when I remembered Octavia; I could hear her making small happy noises somewhere along the corridor, but felt it time I should go and see if she was doing something destructive, like unravelling the frayed end of the hall carpet. She was remarkably persistent in destruction for her age.

I was rather dismayed when I realized she was in Lydia's room and that I must have left the door open, for Lydia's room was always full of nasty objects like aspirins, safety razors and bottles of ink: I rushed along to rescue her and the sight that met my eyes when I opened the door was enough to make anyone quake. She had her back to the door and was sitting in the middle of the floor surrounded by a sea of torn, strewed, chewed paper. I stood there transfixed, watching the neat small back of her head and her thin stalk-like neck and flowery curls: suddenly she gave a great screech of delight and ripped another sheet of paper. "Octavia," I said in horror, and she started guiltily, and looked round at me with a charming deprecating smile: her mouth, I could see, was wedged full of wads of Lydia's new novel.

I picked her up and fished the bits out and laid them carefully on the bedside table with what was left of the typescript; pages 70 to 123 seemed to have survived. The rest was in varying stages of dissolution: some pages were entire but badly crumpled, some were in large pieces, some in small pieces, and some, as I have said, were chewed up. The damage was not, in fact, as great as it appeared at first sight to be, for babies, though persistent, are not thorough: but at first sight it was frightful. I hardly knew where to begin, so I did not begin: I went out and firmly shut the door. Then I carried Octavia back with me into the sitting room, and sat down and thought. In a way it was clearly the most awful thing for which I had ever been responsible, but as I watched Octavia crawl around the sitting room looking for more work to do, I almost wanted to laugh. It seemed so absurd, to have this small living extension of myself, so dangerous, so vulnerable, for whose injuries and crimes I alone had to suffer. It was truly a case of the right hand not seeing what the left hand was doing, for both good and ill. Let my keen knife see not the wound it makes. It really was a terrible thing, I realized this, especially as by constant nattering I had at last persuaded Lydia of the necessity for keeping her door shut: and yet in comparison with Octavia being so sweet and so alive it did not seem so very terrible.

I wondered what to say to Lydia when she returned.

There was one possibility of innocence left to me: I could pretend that she had left the door open herself the day before, for she would surely not recollect her movements clearly enough to dispute the point. This would to a certain extent absolve me: I would thus be guilty of failing to keep an eye on the baby, but not of opening the door to let her in. As a very small child I frequently made this kind of lie, because I found the prospect of admitting guilt so intolerable: which perhaps proves that I feared the smirch on my character more than the crime itself. As an older child, honour always made me confess, and I could see that honour would bring me to it this time. I tried to imagine what she would say. I wondered what I would have said if somebody had ripped up my thesis. I was fairly sure that Lydia never had carbon copies of anything, because I remembered hearing her complain to Joe, who always made three copies of everything, even correspondence, that his attitude bespoke not efficiency but arrogance. I tried to remember whether she had said that she had actually finished the work or not: it had taken her long enough, well over a year, because she had been considerably hampered by the Joe affair. I thought she had reached the last chapter from what she had said last time I had paid her any attention: I wondered if this would make her more or less angry. She had, incidentally, never confessed to the subject matter of this work, and it occurred to me that there was a certain poetic justice in having an exposition of me and Octavia ripped up by Octavia herself.

There was some parallel historic instance of this offense haunting my mind which I could not at first place; I wrote another hundred words on Defoe while trying to remember it, for I knew that it would soothe me if I could recollect. At the end of the hundred words the baby started to moan, so I took her back to her cot for her morning nap, and as I lowered her in over the bars it suddenly came to me. Carlyle's *History of the French Revolution*, that was it. He had lent it to the unfortunate John Stuart Mill to have a quick read, and John Stuart Mill's maid had lit the fire with it. The whole first volume had been completely destroyed, and he had to rewrite the lot. I remembered reading of how Mill and his wife had honourably got in a cab and driven straight off to Carlyle's to confess, but what Carlyle had said I had never discovered. Perhaps history has not recorded his words. This incident had always captured my imagination in a peculiarly forceful way, perhaps because it seemed to be a perfect illustration of an enormous and unwitting wrong done to another, in which the guilt of the agent (carelessness, surely, at most?) bore no relation to the injury sustained by the plaintiff. My mind had always boggled at what Mill had said to Carlyle, at what Carlyle had said to Mill: well, now I had done it. Now I would find out.

I spent the rest of the morning anxiously waiting for the sound of Lydia's key in the door; her movements were always unpredictable, and she might well have arrived at any moment. However, she did not. Octavia and I had our lunch in peace and safety, and after lunch we had to go out to a friend's for tea. I wondered whether or not to leave a note for Lydia, or whether to leave the facts to speak for themselves. In the end I left the facts: I could not think of what to put on a note. We had a very agreeable tea party; my friend had a baby more or less the same age as mine, so the rooms were mercifully devoid of breakable ashtrays, unguarded fires, novels in typescript and other such hazards. My friend had been at Cambridge with me and was now, to her great annoyance, nothing but a wife and mother, and really I felt I was the better off of the two. So cheered was I by an hour or so of comforting literary and maternal and malicious chat that I even recounted, with much gusto, Octavia's awful exploit of the morning, and we both, believe it or not, laughed gaily at what she had done. Sarah was not, however, unimpressed by the gravity of the offense, and when she had stopped laughing she expressed suitable concern over my plight. "What will she say," she said, "what will she say? Will she be angry?"

"I just don't know," I said truthfully. "She never is angry, but then I don't know anyone who is angry. Do you?"

"No, I don't, really," she agreed. "I know people who are angry about people, and behind people's backs, but not anyone who is angry at people. The only person I ever get angry at is my husband."

"If she really is angry," I said, "she might go away and then I wouldn't have anyone to baby-sit for me any more. Not that she does now, very often. But she always will if I catch her in time."

"If you ask me," said Sarah, "it would be a very good thing if she went. Then you could get yourself a proper tenant and charge them a proper rent. It's ridiculous, giving away accommodation in your situation."

"I suppose it is, in a way. But she won't be angry enough to go."

"She might be," said Sarah. "You never know, she might be."

Octavia and I went home by bus, and got back at six. There was still no sign of Lydia. I gave Octavia her bottle and put her to bed, then switched on a concert and sat down to wait. It occurred to me that she and Joe might arrive together, as they frequently did, which would make my confession quite insupportable, for I had always prided myself on regarding Joe from a position of dignity and control. It meant a lot to me, the safety of my attitude. Just after eight, however, Joe phoned and asked if Lydia was in yet; I said not, and was he expecting her to be in. He said that he was, and that she would be arriving shortly, and could I tell her that he'd be round to pick her up at nine, and would she make sure to be changed and ready. The thought of her imminent arrival filled me with sudden panic and I found myself, to my own surprise, starting to relate the whole story once again to Joe. He listened in silence, and when I had finished all he said was:

"Well, well, you really have gone and done it. She's so inefficient, she'll never get round to patching it up. And she loathes rewriting, you know."

"That's very cold comfort," I said. "Will she be very cross?"

"Cross? No, I don't imagine so. Shall I come round straightaway and tell her and hold your hand?"

"No, don't bother, I'd better do it by myself," I said. "I hope you're going somewhere nice this evening, to cheer her up and distract her."

"We were going to a party," he said, "but after a tragedy like this perhaps she won't want to go. I'll take you instead if you like."

"I don't think that would be very tactful," I said.

"No, I suppose not," said Joe. "Never mind. I'll be round at nine to pick up the pieces. Remember exactly what she says for me, will you? I might use it some day."

"So might I," I said. "Or so might she. Let's all write a book about it."

"All right," said Joe. "I'll be seeing you."

"Fine," I said, and rang off. I could not escape the impression that Joe had been distinctly pleased by the news of Lydia's professional setback; he really hated anyone except himself to publish anything, unless it got atrocious reviews and ruined the reputation of its author. I wondered, in view of this, why I liked him. Because I did, and do.

At twenty to nine, Lydia arrived. She rushed in, evidently in a hurry, calling in the sitting room only to say that she had to go out again quick. Feeling a little sick, I followed her along the corridor to her room and arrested her at the door by saying feebly:

"Joe rang."

"Oh, did he?" she said, her hand on the knob. "What for?"

"He said to tell you he'd be round for you at nine."

"Oh hell," said Lydia. "I'm late, I know," and she started to turn the knob.

"Lydia," I said bravely, "Lydia, the most terrible thing happened today. Really terrible. I don't know how to explain to you."

"What do you mean?" she said, turning to me and turning the knob at the same time, so that the door opened, revealing the mess within to me but not to her. I realized that there was no need to put my offense into words, so I pointed to the scraps of paper and said:

"Look. Just look at that. Octavia did it."

She looked. I was curiously satisfied, on some level, that she actually blenched. She said nothing at all but went in and started to inspect the damage, picking up a few of the more undestroyed sheets and putting them on the bedside table, with a bemused expression on her face. Then she gave up but did not look at me.

"I'm so sorry," I said. "I can't tell you how upset I am. It's all my fault, I went into your room this morning to see if you were there, to tell you something, and I must have left the door open. I don't remember, but I must have done. And Octavia got in. I can't tell you how sorry I am."

She sat down on the bed, weakly. I thought for a moment she was going to cry, but she didn't. She said, after a long pause,

"Oh dear. Never mind, I suppose I can patch it together again."

"I didn't touch it," I said, "after I'd found it. I thought I might do more harm than good."

"You mean you didn't look at it? You didn't read any of it?" she said, with some faint growing signs of animation.

"No, no," I assured her. "Not at all. I just shut the door. I was so horrified."

"Oh well, that's just as well," she said. Then she knelt down amongst the scraps and said, quite cheerfully:

"I'm sure I can put it together again. And if I do have to rewrite a few bits, that'll be good for me, because things are always better the second time, I'm just too lazy to do it, that's all. It'll probably be good for me, going through it again."

She started to pick up the bits, trying to put them in numerical order: I stood in the doorway watching her. After a moment or two she lost patience and said:

"Oh God, I can't be bothered with it now, I'd better get changed or Joe'll come and be angry with me. He's got a frightful temper, Joe has."

And she started to undo her mackintosh and then took off her skirt and jersey and wandered over to the wardrobe in her petticoat and started to look for something to wear.

She might have been able to leave it at that, but I was not.

"Lydia," I said, "I've been thinking. It can't be much fun for you living here with the baby all over the place, baby food and crying at night, and then awful things like this. Don't you think you ought to move?"

"I hadn't thought of it," said Lydia, getting down a strange gold lurex jersey top and starting to pull it over her head. "I really haven't noticed the baby, I mean except when I baby-sit for you. I think she's lovely."

"But she's such a nuisance," I said. "And when she starts to walk, it'll be worse. I won't be able to keep her out of anywhere."

"Are you trying to get rid of me?" said Lydia, trying on a black fringed skirt and discarding it in favour of a full-length purple wool one. Her petticoat, once lemon yellow, was now an amazing shade of grey, and full of holes and ladders.

"Of course not," I said. "I just thought you might not want to go on staying here, that's all."

"Well, I'll have to go when your parents come back anyway," said Lydia. "But till then I'd much rather stay here. I like it here. Where else could I go?"

"You could go to Joe's," I said.

"Oh God, no," said Lydia, wrinkling her nose in horror. "It's so dirty there. It smells. You should just see what he keeps under his bed. Perhaps you have seen what he keeps under his bed."

She started to put her hair up into its familiar droopy, straying evening chignon, and I reflected, not for the first time, that she and Joe had an uncanny physical similarity, for they both looked dirty and shabby from close to, yet both had a great degree of loose objective and not purely contemporary beauty. Lydia never looked clean; her skin was not pitted like Joe's but it had a permanent greyness, the greyness of one reared on baked beans, jelly and bread and dripping. They both looked unhealthy, whereas I have the hard fit shine of the well-nurtured. Lydia did wash from time to time, for I had seen and heard her do so; she washed her clothes, too, but perhaps not quite often enough. Since Octavia's birth I had become more conscious of dirt and washing myself, and had even started to think of Lydia's aspect with mild reprehension.

When she turned round from her mirror she looked beautiful all right, though in her usual tawdry way.

"What's the time?" she said. "Have I time to put some make-up on before Joe comes?"

"It's five to," I said.

She turned back to her mirror. "I do overdress, don't I?" she said as she started to slap on a little foundation.

"Lydia," I said firmly, trying to pull her back to my preoccupation. "Do you really want to stay?"

"Of course I do," she said. "It's so handy for me here."

"I suppose you can, then," I said. "Because my parents aren't coming back. Not for another year."

"Really?" She turned round, evidently delighted. "I say that's wonderful. How did you persuade them to stay away?"

"I didn't," I said. "They just wrote and said they were staying."

"How marvellous." She turned back and put on some lipstick, then, with her back still towards me, said:

"I say, Rosamund, you didn't rip up my book on purpose, did you? To try to get rid of me?"

"What?" I said, righteously indignant. "What a fantastic notion. Of course I didn't. Whatever could have given you such an idea?"

"Oh, nothing, nothing," said Lydia. "No, I know you wouldn't do a thing like that. Can I really stay?"

"If you really want to," I said, kindly, magnanimously, and at that Joe rang the bell. I went to answer it; Joe was slightly drunk and kissed me with warm affection when I let him in.

"What did she say?" he said.

"I'll tell you later," I said, and Lydia appeared, gaily painted, the stray cheek curls of her hair matted with accidental pink foundation and little dusty pools of powder in the corners of her large eyes.

"Isn't it wonderful?" she said, as she joined us. "That I can stay?"

"What do you mean?" said Joe, and I had to explain once more about my parents not coming back, and we all had a drink to celebrate, which Joe actually went out to buy as I was too poor that month for alcohol. Then they went off to their party, and that was it, except for the fact that Lydia really did have to rewrite two whole chapters as well as doing a lot of boring sellotaping, and when it came out it got bad reviews anyway. This did succeed in making

Lydia angry; she stormed up and down for several hours, grimly abusing the private lives, education and affinities of her critics, and when I pointed out that she was bound to get bad reviews sooner or later she stormed at me too, and would not forgive me for a long time. Joe was naturally delighted with her notices, though from a distance, as he and Lydia had by then parted forever, and now never met; though I still saw him, infrequently, for an incestuous friendship will outlive, as I have discovered, any passionate love.

It was the night before Christmas that I met George. The circumstances have an indelible beauty, like the beauty of fate itself. It did not seem so at the time, for confusion obscured their strange outlines, but now in retrospect I feel that I could reconsider forever the paths I walked along, the bonds that bound me.

Beatrice had invited me to spend Christmas with them, but I had declined. She wanted to see Octavia, she said, but Octavia belonged to me and to London and I did not want to disperse and diffuse her over family and countryside. More strangely, Clare and Andrew invited me as well; courtesy dies hard. Their invitation too I declined, for I did not wish ever to see them again. I felt sad that they should have felt so sorry for me, my brother and my sister, especially as I was in good spirits; I had been offered a good job for the following autumn at one of the most attractive new universities, my thesis was at the publisher's, and on the strength of it my name was in considerable esteem amongst those in a position to esteem it. I was gratified and relieved; I had known all along that it was an exceptional piece of work, and fully deserved any attention it might attract, and yet at the same time I was half expecting it to go unnoticed, as so many others had gone before it. In my general academic goodwill I had gratuitously embarked on a piece of work on Cowley, and had also been invited to write, for considerable remuneration, a chapter in a paperback survey of poetry; so I had good cause for my high spirits. It was gratifying, too, that my name would in the near future be Dr. Rosamund Stacey, a form of address which would go a long way towards obviating the anomaly of Octavia's existence.

I spent the afternoon of December 24th in the British Museum; I had no worries about the morrow, as Lydia had arranged to cook a turkey for me and had invited dozens of her friends to come and eat it. I like Lydia's parties, especially the ones she holds in my flat, for I do not have to worry about baby-sitters for them, nor getting to bed after them. Lydia is also quite a good cook when she gets going, though bizarre: I am much better at making food edible, but she is excellent at making it amazing, rich and rare. She is usually successful if her ingredients are good enough, and I felt it would take a lot of ill-combined herbs and wine and mashed chestnuts to ruin, right through, a whole large turkey. So I sat there peacefully enough, reading Johnson's views on Cowley, and thinking that perhaps I might move on to Johnson and the eighteenth century next, in a year or two's time. Anything seemed interesting that afternoon; such moods are not common. On the way out, at half past four, everyone wished me a Merry Christmas, and I wished it back to them; I like cloakroom attendants who stay in cloakrooms, librarians who stay in libraries, doormen who stay at doors. It is only when they follow me down the street that I panic.

On the way home I even remembered to buy a Christmas present for Mrs. Jennings, who had reminded me of my obligation by producing hers for Octavia before I left. It was a nice rolling ball with a bell inside. I bought her a box of soap and perfume, and rushed home with it; when I got back, Mrs. Jennings thanked me for the present and said that Octavia had played with the ball, but that she seemed a little cross, and that her nose was running a lot. I looked at her and, sure enough, her nose was running.

"It's nothing very much," said Mrs. Jennings, as soon as she could see that she had alarmed me. "Just a sniffle. Teething, I expect."

"Yes, I expect it is," I agreed.

"She probably caught it from me," said Mrs. Jennings. "I had a shocking sore throat when I came on Monday, but I didn't want to upset you."

"Oh, that's all right," I said.

"Merry Christmas, then," said Mrs. Jennings, and after I had persuaded the baby to wave her good-bye she departed, and I was left to consider the severity of her cold. It did not, I had to admit, seem very bad, yet it was definitely there, and it had not been there that morning when I had left. I looked at my watch; it was after five. I wondered whether I ought to go down to the chemist's and get her some penicillin, for which I had a permanent prescription from Protheroe, but decided against it, for I had nowhere to leave Octavia while I went and could not possibly take her out in the evening in such icy weather. So I decided to pretend I had not noticed, and continued as usual, giving her her bottle and cereal, and playing with her, and putting her to bed, though omitting her bath. She did, as Mrs. Jennings had remarked, seem a little cross, but no worse than cross, and she went to bed quietly and without a murmur, as ever.

I then proceeded to get on with my evening's work: I washed my hair, as a gesture towards the festivities of the morrow, and then sat down by the fire to straighten out my correspondence and income tax, which had accumulated into a mess of staggering proportions. I had a good deal of information about what concessions I was or was not allowed as an unmarried mother, tax-wise, and was just discovering to my great indignation that I really could not get Mrs. Jennings' wages allowed, when I heard Octavia cough. Nothing much: just once. I went to have a look at her, and she was lying there peacefully enough, breathing her quiet baby sleep; her nose was no longer running, and was not even very blocked. As I watched, she stirred and coughed again. It was so mild, so gentle a noise, so like a clearing of the throat, that I knew I should not take it seriously; I knew it was nothing. And yet responsibility lay so heavy on me that I could not take what I knew to be the truth. The thought of a long, doctorless Christmas, without penicillin, oppressed me beyond all reason; I could not bear the thought that any however trifling or permissible negligence of mine should ever cause her any possibility of harm. I would have to go for the penicillin, I realized, even if reason reasserted itself once I had got it, for I suspected that I would decide, if I had it in the flat, that it would not be worth waking her to administer it. And yet, not having it, I had to go. I went out of her bedroom and looked at my watch; it was after eight.

As luck would have it, I lived within ten minutes' walk of one of the only all-night, every-night chemists in London, John Bell and Croydon, on Wigmore Street. The thought of their proximity had comforted me more than once, though the most I had ever purchased there had been a thermometer and a bottle of codeine. However, near as it was, I did not like the idea of leaving Octavia unattended at night in the flat. Even though I was leaving her for a mere twenty minutes, and for her own good at that. Even though she never woke in the evening. Even though, even if she woke, she could not do anything but cry, and crying for twenty minutes never hurt anyone. She could come to no possible harm, I said to myself, and yet I was not capable of leaving her.

I went back into the sitting room, and tried to work out why I was so reluctant to go. There must, I thought, be some rational basis for my fears; or some irrational basis, come to that. I had a dim feeling that it was actually illegal to leave small children unattended in houses after dark, though I knew that this suspicion was gleaned from a stray remark in a modern novel, for which I could have given chapter and verse: hardly the strongest of legal authorities. And even if there were such an unlikely law, it could scarcely be stretched to apply to my particular situation. So what, then, did I fear? Did I just fear, meaninglessly, for the sake of it? Had I got as far as that in the decay of sense? Had so strong a pattern of apprehension been set up in me that it could never now be broken by character or will? I did not believe it, I did not wish to believe it, and I sat there for five minutes before I worked out the answer. Supposing, I said to myself, just supposing, that while I am out the block of flats should catch fire. If it did, I would be out, and nobody but I would know that Octavia was there, and so nobody would bother to rescue her, and by the time I got back it might be too late. This is what I said to myself, and it seemed reasonable enough. I was not cut out for responsibility, but I do my best.

Having thus finally, like a cat, triumphantly cornered my small mouse-like elusive fear, I knew at once what I would have to do about it, distasteful though it might be. So there is some point in thinking, though I sometimes doubt it. I would have to go round to one of my neighbours and tell them that I was going, and that they must rescue the baby if there was a fire. I shrink abnormally from appeals for assistance, and yet this would have to be done; I wondered which of my neighbours I should select. The couple across the corridor were evidently unsuitable, being themselves extremely old and frail and foreign. Beneath me lived two possibilities; in one flat there was an opera singer and his mistress, and in the other a chilly, disagreeable-looking man of no clear profession, his well-permed wife, and his superior teen-age son. I had never had any truck with either of these ménages, and neither had my parents before me, as far as I knew; the opera singer and his mistress looked good-natured enough, yet somehow indefinably unreliable, whereas the other family looked positively ill-natured and thoroughly dependable. The one lot always smiled in the lift or on the stairs, but the other never; the only words that the well-permed wife had ever spoken to me had been a request to hold the lift door open for her when her arms were too full of Harrods' parcels to do it herself. It had not been a very graciously worded request, either, I remembered. Nevertheless, I felt that I must approach these first, if only because they looked, as I have said, dependable.

I put on my hat and coat and took a last look at Octavia, who was sleeping as though nothing could rouse her; then I went downstairs, leaving the door on the latch. I rang the bell of the dependable family, and the man answered with remarkable promptness; he seemed to have been waiting for it to ring. As indeed he had; from noises within, I could tell that they were having a party.

"Excuse me," I said nervously, peering past him into his flowery papered hall, "I'm from the flat upstairs, I wondered if I could possibly ask you a favour."

"Come in, come in," said the ill-natured-looking man cheerily, "come in and let us know what we can do."

"Oh no, I can't come *in*," I said, "I was just going out for a few moments, I have to go down to the chemist's, and the thing is, I have to leave the baby alone for a few minutes, and I wondered if you could possibly . . ." I hesitated, not knowing what they could possibly do . . . "if you could possibly just keep an eye on her?"

"Certainly, certainly," he said, more jovially than ever. "I'll get my wife to pop up and have a look at her, shall I?"

"Oh no, there's no need for that," I said hastily, "there's no need to *do* anything, there's no need to go to any trouble. She won't wake, I know she won't wake, she never does. It's just in case."

I didn't like to say, bluntly, just in case the house catches fire, it sounded so silly, but astonishingly he took the words out of my mouth.

"All right," he said, "don't you worry, if the place goes up in smoke, I'll go and rescue her myself."

"Oh, thank you,' I said, "thank you so much. I won't be a minute, I just didn't want to leave her and nobody knowing she was there . . . I left the door unlocked; that's so very nice of you."

I was about to start backing humbly away when the man's wife materialized in the background, whereupon he started to recount to her the whole story. She was looking gay and cheery, a basket-shaped brooch of diamonds sparkling on her dark green lapel, and she too started to assure me of her earnest solicitude.

"I'll pop up myself," she said, "and just have a little listen, shall I?"

"There's no need," I said once more.

"And how is your little baby?" she went on, "she's been so ill, hasn't she? I was so worried about you both, and I *was* glad when she came back again safe and sound. She's quite well again now, is she?"

"Oh yes, quite well," I said, then added for good measure, "I just have to be careful with her, that's all."

"Oh yes, of course," said the woman knowingly, as though she knew every detail of my afflictions.

"I must get off to the chemist's now," I said, and started to edge away; this precipitated a renewed flow of invitation from them both, who begged me to come in for a drink, to come and join the party when I got back. So astonished was I that I think I might have accepted had I not been conscious that my hair inside my hat was still wet from its washing, for I doubted if they would continue to take me to their bosoms if I confronted them with it. So I said good night and thanked them for their kindness, and they wished me a Merry Christmas, and I wished them one, and so we parted. As I went down the remaining floors in the lift, I wondered why they had been so obliging, and the thought crossed my mind that they must both have been a little drunk; but it occurred to me later that it was largely the fact that I had asked them a favour that had so warmed their demeanour. I had admitted need, and there is no prospect so warming as the sight of another's need, when we can supply it without effort to ourselves. I do not belittle their kindness, for they were kind, and the woman had been genuinely concerned about Octavia, though how or why she had interested herself in the matter I cannot imagine; for it is true that ever after this evening they treated me with the greatest kindliness and consideration, asking after the baby and my work, and even buying a copy of my book and asking me to autograph it for them when it finally emerged, though sixteenth-century poetry can hardly have been their favourite reading matter. They bought it through sheer kindness to me, as they asked me in for a drink that Christmas Eve. If I asked more favours of people, I would find people more kind.

It was cold and slightly foggy out; the parked cars were gleaming with a thin layer of frost. I walked briskly, for I did not wish to be long. I was feeling happy rather than not, cheered that I had so successfully braved my neighbours, and confident now I was on the move that Octavia was suffering from no more than teeth and a slight snuffle. I like going to all-night chemists, for they share the irregular glamour of all-night cafés, bars, airports and launderettes. There was a queue inside when I got there, inevitably I suppose, so I queued in the gloomy light, then handed in my prescription, then went to sit down and wait while it was made up. In the center of the large dim waiting room there is a tank of tropical fish, surrounded by a circular bench; I sat and watched the fish, endlessly and soothingly drifting around their glass cage, and I wondered if fish ever sleep. I watched them for some minutes, and then, just as I looked away, I heard somebody say "Rosa-mund," and I looked up, and it was George.

He was standing over me, smiling gently and diffidently, and I tried to rise to my feet but my legs would not hold me. I think I did not speak quickly enough, though I did finally manage to say:

"Why, it's George."

For so long now I had not seen him that I was bereft of all power, so great was my amazement, so many my thoughts, so troubled my heart. I sat there, dumb, and looked at him, and my mouth smiled, for I was terrified that he would go once more and leave me, that he was on his way elsewhere, that he would not wish to stop. I wanted to detain him: I wanted to say, stay with me, but my mouth was so dry I could not speak. So I gazed at him and smiled.

"Rosamund," he said. "It's so long since I saw you, I thought you must have moved. It must be two years since I saw you."

"Almost," I said.

"Are you waiting for something?" he asked, and I nodded and whispered, "Yes, I'm waiting for a prescrip-tion."

"I'm waiting too," he said, and sat down by my side. He sat there by me and of his own free will. I recovered, very slightly, the power of speech, and I said:

"Are you ill, then?"

"No, I'm not ill," he said, "not really ill. I've got this bad throat, that's all. I have to get some things for it."

"You're working over Christmas, are you?" I asked.

"That's right," he said.

"I knew you hadn't moved," I said, "although I hadn't seen you. I hear you on the radio. I knew you must still be there."

"I did see you once, actually," he said, "but I couldn't speak to you. It was on the tube, you were in a different carriage, but I could just see you through the glass doors. I waved but you wouldn't look."

"I didn't see you," I said.

"I thought you didn't."

We both fell silent once more and I began to think that it was about time that my prescription might be ready.

"I'd better go," I said, "and see if my thing's done."

"You're not ill, are you?" he said, and then added quickly, so that I need not answer, "Not that one should *ever* ask a lady what she wants in a *chemist's*, I'm quite well aware of that."

"No, I'm not ill," I said, and stood up, and stood there looking down at him, and the coloured fish swimming patiently behind his narrow head.

"You're not in a hurry, are you, Rosamund?" he then said. "We could go and have a drink somewhere, couldn't we? To celebrate Christmas?"

I paused, strung delightfully onto the future, connected for an instant by hope of what was to come.

"I can't come and have a drink," I said, and then went on, partly to excuse myself and partly to pave the way for further negotiation, "I have to get back to the baby, you see."

I had made this excuse so often to others that I did not realize its import in such a place to such a person; I had not meant to reveal myself in this way, though how else I had never satisfactorily considered.

"You've got a baby, have you," said George. "I didn't even know you were married."

"I'm not," I said, and smiled, this time with true confidence; for here I was, safely back in my old role, the girl with alternating lovers, the girl with stray babies, the girl who does what she wants and does not suffer for it. He took it, as ever before, wonderfully as I offered it, and he pulled a face and said in his most camp tones, camp, vulgar, lady-like tones, that filled me with extreme delight:

"I say, Rosamund, you *are* a one."

"It's a very nice baby," I continued, gaiety mounting irresistibly in my heart.

"I'm sure it is," he said. "Any baby of yours must be quite delightful, I'm sure of that."

"Why don't you come round and have a look at her?" I said. "Come round for a drink. I've got to get back because there's no one else in the flat, but it would be nice if you would come."

I knew he would accept, from the way he was looking at me, or I would not have asked.

"I should be most happy to come," he said. "How nice of you to ask me. After all this time."

And he looked at me, oblique, slanted, his words full of implications yet so mild and harmless, so much on my side, so little against me, so little a threat that I felt weak with relief. I thought, looking at him, that he was almost very handsome; with a little more weight he might have been a handsome man.

"You're looking very beautiful tonight, Rosamund," he said, speaking, I felt, as I was listening, only for the pleasure of it. "More beautiful than ever, if I may say so."

"It's so dark in here," I said, "that you can't possibly tell. By daylight I look haggard."

"Do you really? I'm beginning to look rather old myself."

"I don't think you would ever look old," I said. "You've not got the kind of face that gets old."

"You can't see," he said, "in this light."

"I must go and collect my prescription. It must be ready by now. Wait for me."

"You'll have to wait for me," he said. "Mine isn't ready yet. Come back and wait with me."

"All right," I said. I would always rather wait than be awaited. So I went up to the counter and collected Octavia's penicillin, then went back to sit and wait with George.

"How old is your baby?" was the first thing that he said to me when I returned. Quickly, surprisingly quickly for one so bad at dates, I realized that it would be better and less committing to give a wrong age, so I lied and said that she was eleven months old, although she was still a long way off this ripe age. As soon as I had said it, I wondered if I had done the right thing, for it would be difficult to retract should I ever wish to do so; also, if Octavia really had been eleven months old, then I would have been already pregnant when I had slept with George. The whole business was too complicated for me; the truth seemed somewhere during the intervening months to have lost itself forever. I looked at George, and wondered if it had ever really happened; he did not look capable of it, he looked as mild and frail and non-masculine as he had appeared at our first meeting, when I had been so sure that it was Joe he fancied. I had had this sensation of disbelief before with other men, though to a lesser degree, naturally; Hamish, for instance, my first love, I had met after a couple of years' total absence, since when I had seen him frequently, for he, too, worked in the British Museum from time to time. The first time I saw him I had been shocked and amazed, for we had parted on poor terms, but after a coffee together we had quickly established an acquaintance from which to discuss poets and old friends. I had never, however, managed to get over the fact that we had once known and loved each other so thoroughly; sitting talking to him and his wife over coffee and Danish pastries, I would suddenly be assailed by sharp memories of his lips and teeth and naked flesh. They were not memories of desire, for I no longer desired him; rather they were shocking, anti-social disruptive memories, something akin to those impulses to strip oneself in crowded tube trains, to throw oneself from theater balconies.

Images of fear, not of desire. Other people do not feel this way about old lovers, I know. It must be just another instance of my total maladjustment with regard to sex.

When George had collected his pills for his throat, we set off back towards the flat. It was too cold to walk slowly, and when I walk quickly I have not enough breath left for talking, so we did not talk. In the lift on the way up to my floor, George suddenly said:

"I kept thinking I would see you, but I never did."

I wondered if this was said as apology or as accusation, but it was impossible from his tone to tell. Like me, he veiled his intention until there was nothing of it left.

"You really didn't know about my baby?" I said, as a rejoinder.

"How should I have known?" he said. "Who would have told me?" And I realized another factor in our delicate situation; if indeed he assumed that I had been pregnant at the time of our last fatal encounter, then that would have been an excellent reason for my not having wanted to go on seeing him. Regardless of him, and whether I liked him and what he had done to me. And assuming that the avoidance had truly been more on my side than on his. Assuming so many things. I shook my head to myself, sadly bewildered, and opened the lift door. I wished above anything that I could know what he thought. I would have liked to have looked inside his head and seen what was going on there. But who knows, there may have been the same dependent, interlocking uncertain confusion in his head as in mine, and no enlightenment at all.

I spent a long time looking for my doorkey, as I had forgotten that I had left the door unlocked. When I finally remembered and pushed it open, I left George in the sitting room while I went to look at Octavia, who was still sleeping sweetly, and with now no trace of either cold or cough. I wondered if I should take George to see her. I wondered if the call of blood would reveal to him as in a fairy story that she was his child. I thought not. I do not know whether at that moment I meant to tell him; I think I did not, I think I was waiting to see what became of us both. I tucked her blue airy blankets in more closely and went back to George. He was sitting looking at the proofs of an article of mine on an article on a book on Spenser and courtly love, and he looked up at me as I entered and said:

"You seem to do quite a lot of writing these days. I see things with your name on quite often."

"Do you really?" I said, surprised, for I very rarely published anything in any publication with a circulation outside the profession. "You must read a lot," I said.

"Yes, I suppose I do," he said, and left it at that.

"I have to write now," I said, "for the money. I used to try not to, I don't really approve of that kind of thing, but money is money. It keeps her in zinc and castor oil ointment. They make one do a lot of things, babies, that one doesn't really approve of."

I went over to the corner cupboard and started to get out Lydia's Christmas drink and some glasses. There was a new bottle of whisky; I poured us both a glass and went to sit down.

"It suits you, having a baby," he said. "You look well on it. Even in proper electric light."

"I'm glad you think so."

"I saw Joe Hurt not so long ago. You still see something of him?"

"Quite a lot, one way and another. He's going out with the girl who shares my flat."

"Oh, really. You've gone off him, have you?"

"I was never really on him, to tell you the truth." I might as well, after all, tell him a bit of the truth, I thought. "Not really. I like him, though."

"You never used to share the flat. You had it to yourself."

"There again, you see, things have altered. I had to take a lodger. For the baby-sitting."

"And for the money."

"Yes, and for the money. Though I'm not too badly off, you know." And lest he should form any lurid pictures of my financial plight, I started to tell him about my thesis, and my new job, and my bright prospects. Having told him about the progress of my career, I felt entitled to ask him about his, so I did, but he proved as cagey as ever.

"Oh, I'm still doing more or less the same routine," he said evasively, in answer to my queries.

"Why don't you have a change?" I said, unable to prevent myself. "Why don't you do something different? Aren't you bored?"

"You said that last time I saw you," he said. "I don't see why I should be bored. For what it is, my job is extremely well paid. I don't see why I should change."

"You could get a job on the television," I said. "That must be better paid, isn't it?"

"Not spectacularly," said George. "And anyway, I don't want to be on the television."

"You'd be so good on the television," I said, unable to let the notion drop. "You'd look so wonderful on the television. You've got just the right kind of face for it, all lean and bony. You'd look wonderful on it. Then I could sit and watch you as well as hearing you."

I meant this, too, although he could never have guessed it; I would have liked to have done just that.

"I don't really want to be on the television," he repeated patiently. "It makes your life a misery, that machine. Wherever you go, you pay for it. Why are you so keen for me to be on it?"

"I told you," I said truthfully. "So I could sit and watch you."

"Well, why don't you go and be on it then? And then I could sit and watch you."

"*I* don't want to be on it," I said. "I have all sorts of far more important things to do."

"So have I," said George. "You're not the only one with a life of your own, you know."

Silence fell between us; I drank another mouthful of whisky and wondered what to do. There seemed to be some deadlock between us that could never be broken, for neither of us was given to breaking such things, so we might well sit there forever estranged, forever connected. I would not have minded if it could have been there that we could have stayed, but I knew that a connection so tenuous could not last, could not remain frozen and entranced forever, but must melt if so left, from the mere mortal warmth of continuing life. If one of us did not move towards the other, then we could only move apart. Like two fish, embalmed in the living frozen river, we eyed each other in silence through the solid resistant intervening air, and did not move. After a while, when silence itself threatened to become some kind of positive action, he spoke.

"Your hair," he said, "your hair is turning grey."

I raised a hand to my head and nodded, for it was true.

"It must be worry," I said. "Worry has driven me to it."

"What do you worry about?" he said with a gentleness that ignored the flippancy of my answer, and responded more to the white threads in my hair.

"Everything," I said, "everything."

"Tell me," he said.

"There's nothing to tell," I said, and thought of Octavia. Despite myself, I began to remember; I remembered how often I had reached for the phone, in those first months, to ring Broadcasting House and ask for George; how consciously I had restrained myself from going to the pub to see him, from walking the streets he might walk; how I had lain in bed at the hospital and listened through my institution earphones for his voice, how I had wept and lain awake and wished to share the misery of my child's affliction and the joy of her joy, how I had endured and survived and spared him so much sorrow, and I thought that now I did not see how I could go back on what I had done.

"It was nothing," I said. "The baby was rather ill, but she's better now."

"I'm sorry about that," said George. "What was it, was it serious?"

"No, nothing serious," I said. "I just worry about everything, that's all."

"You must have had a bad time," said George. "You've lost weight. But it suits you."

"Oh, I can't complain," I said. "Others are worse off than me, aren't they? Why should I complain? Don't let me complain, tell me about you instead."

"There's nothing to tell," said George, "of any interest. I haven't had too good a year, but it's over now. Tell me about you. I'm more interested in you. Have your parents come back from Africa yet? They were in Africa, weren't they?"

"No, they haven't come back, they're going to India instead. They were supposed to be coming back, but they changed their minds and went to India."

"How do they like it there?"

"I don't know. They've only just gone."

"They get around, don't they?" said George. "I was thinking of going abroad myself."

"What for?"

"Oh, I don't know," said George, smiling down into his glass. "Just for a change. To get away. To see what turns up. There's nothing to keep me."

And he looked up at me, and I had the sense that I so often had with him, that he was on the verge of some confession, some confidence, some approach that once made could never be denied. And I, for my part, felt myself almost capable of such a scene as I had made in the hospital, when more civilized communication had there failed me; I felt myself on the verge of tears and noise, and I held hard onto the arms of my chair to prevent myself from throwing myself on my knees in front of him, to beseech from him his affection, his tolerance, his pity, anything that would keep him there with me, and save me from being so much alone with my income tax forms, from lacking him so much. Words kept forming inside my head, into phrases like I love you, George, don't leave me, George. I wondered what would happen if I let one of them out into the air. I wondered how much damage it would do.

"What part of the world were you thinking of going to?" I said.

"Oh, I shan't really go," he said. "I was just thinking of going."

"I wouldn't want to go abroad," I said.

"I didn't ask you," he said, "but you can come with me, if you want."

"Can I really?" I emptied my glass. "And can I bring Octavia with me too? I couldn't go anywhere without Octavia."

"Not even with me?" said George.

"Not even with you," I said.

"I don't see why you shouldn't bring her," he said, "though I don't know anything about babies."

"My baby is a nice baby," I said. "She's a very pretty baby."

"How could she not be pretty?" he said, "with such a mother? And I like her name, too. It's a nice name, Octavia."

"I like it," I said, "though a lot of people don't. I called her after Octavia Hill."

"Octavia Hill," he said, "who was she? Wasn't she one of those heroines of feminism and socialism?"

"To tell you the truth," I said, admitting it for the first time, "I'm not quite sure exactly what she *did*, and once I'd chosen the name I didn't dare go and look her up in case she was unsuitable, or famous for something frightful. I think she was a socialist. I hope she was a socialist. Though I don't suppose it matters much, does it?"

"I don't suppose so," he said. "You'll bring her up the right way, won't you, whatever the other one did?"

"I don't know about the right way," I said. "It was right, I suppose, the way I was brought up, but it didn't do me much good, did it?"

"I don't know," said George. "You seem to have done all right, you seem to have done as well as anyone."

"How do you mean?" I said.

"Well," he said, "by your own accounts, you've got a nice job, and a nice baby. What more could anyone want?"

"Some people might want a nice husband too," I said.

"But not you, surely?" said George. "You never seemed to want a husband."

"No," I said, "perhaps I never did. Though I sometimes think it might be easier, to have one. It would be nice to have someone to fill in my income tax forms, for instance," and I pointed despairingly at the mess of papers laid out on the hearth rug.

"You can't have everything," said George.

"No, indeed," I said. "And I have more than most people, I admit."

"So do I," said George, "so do I. Though I, too, have my moments of weakness. Sometimes I feel it would be nice to have someone to iron my shirts. But then, you see, of course I know that I can always do it myself. As well as anyone else could. Just as you can probably make more sense of your income tax than most men could. So it's no argument, really, is it?"

We smiled at each other, feebly, overcast.

"Why don't you come and have a look at my baby?" I said.

"Wouldn't it waken her?" he said, reluctant.

"She never wakes," I said, and I led him along the corridor for my amusement and not for his, and opened the door of her room. There she lay, her eyes closed, her fists sweetly composed upon the pillow, and I looked from her face to George, and I acknowledged that it was too late, much much too late. It was no longer in me to feel for anyone what I felt for my child; compared with the perplexed fitful illuminations of George, Octavia shone there with a faint, constant and pearly brightness quite strong enough to eclipse any more garish future blaze. A bad investment, I knew, this affection, and one that would leave me in the dark and the cold in years to come; but then what warmer passion ever lasted longer than six months?

"She's beautiful," said George.

"Yes, isn't she?" I said.

But it was these words of apparent agreement that measured our hopeless distance, for he had spoken for my sake and I because it was the truth. Love had isolated me more securely than fear, habit or indifference. There was one thing in the world that I knew about, and that one thing was Octavia. I had lost the taste for half-knowledge. George, I could see, knew nothing with such certainty. I neither envied nor pitied his indifference, for he was myself, the self that but for accident, but for fate, but for chance, but for womanhood, I would still have been.

He followed me back along the corridor to the sitting room and there I asked him if he would have another drink. But I asked him in such a way that he would refuse, and he refused.

"I must be going now," he said. "I start work very early in the morning."

"Do you?" I said.

"It was nice to see you again," he said. "Look after yourself, won't you?" And he moved towards the door.

"Yes," I said, "I'll look after myself. Let me know if you do go away. If you go abroad."

"I'll let you know," he said. "And you, don't you worry so much."

"I can't help worrying," I said. "It's my nature. There's nothing I can do about my nature, is there?"

"No," said George, his hand upon the door. "No, nothing."